Conversations with Myself

Short Introspective Discussions About Life

MICHAEL WILLIAM PETERSON

iUniverse

CONVERSATIONS WITH MYSELF
SHORT INTROSPECTIVE DISCUSSIONS ABOUT LIFE

iUniverse books may be ordered through booksellers or by contacting:

iUniverse
1663 Liberty Drive
Bloomington, IN 47403
www.iuniverse.com
1-800-Authors (1-800-288-4677)

Because of the dynamic nature of the Internet, any web addresses or links contained in this book may have changed since publication and may no longer be valid. The views expressed in this work are solely those of the author and do not necessarily reflect the views of the publisher, and the publisher hereby disclaims any responsibility for them.

Any people depicted in stock imagery provided by Getty Images are models, and such images are being used for illustrative purposes only.
Certain stock imagery © Getty Images.

ISBN: 978-1-5320-8702-8 (sc)
ISBN: 978-1-5320-8704-2 (hc)
ISBN: 978-1-5320-8703-5 (e)

Library of Congress Control Number: 2019920603

Print information available on the last page.

iUniverse rev. date: 12/23/2019

For Patti – truly a saint for putting up with all of
my idiosyncrasies and weirdness

Contents

Contents

Introduction

By way of introduction, let me say that all of my life I have considered the art and science of writing as something far beyond the reach of an ordinary man such as myself. I was 17, and living in Kettering, Ohio, when I first attempted to seriously write something other than my assignments for my senior year in high school. When I finished, I had about ten hand-written pages about a senior in high school whose family had moved him his senior year to not only a different high school, or a different city, but to an entirely different state. As you can imagine, my story was somewhat passionate and disturbing as it was based upon my experiences in a completely new, and unwanted, environment. As I read through what I had written, I became discouraged because it was probably what I demonstrated to my parents, and I decided that was not fair.

So, I tore the brilliantly written pages into shreds, and set about to enjoy my senior year in high school. And I did. I became a member of the varsity wrestling team and was able to make some good friends in the school. I learned the main lesson that I feel my father intended for me to learn, i.e, that no matter where you are placed or what is happening, you have the capability of handling the situation if you be what you are, not what others expect you to be. Sort of like Victor Frankl's idea in *Man's Search For Meaning* but situated in a high school and not in a German prison camp, although there probably are some distinct similarities.

After high school I went to college, then got an M.B.A. in Finance and Investments, and thought I was all set to set the business world on fire. My first job was as a salesman of securities for a very well-known brokerage firm in a large city. I did not like it one bit. I loved the industry, but I did not like the idea of selling, or should I say I did not like the idea, or process, of finding new clients or setting up appointments. In retrospect, the idea of talking on the phone to me is repulsive, and therefore my choice of a career at that point was ridiculous.

I know what you are going to say…why did you take the job if you did not like the process?

The answer is simple. My father was a salesman, and I wanted to be just like my dad. I mean that with complete sincerity. I consider my father to be one of the greatest men I have ever met, and in the course of my life I have met quite a few men, both poor and rich, famous and not-so-famous, good and evil, etc. I still consider my dad as the best man I have had the privilege of knowing. I hope I have succeeded in becoming as good a man as he was. That is why I chose to be a salesman.

Having realized my error, I worked at some odd jobs as I went back to school and studied accounting. I love numbers. They make sense, where sometimes people, and their assumptions, do not. I got a job as an entry level accountant and spent the next 30 years moving up the corporate ladder, finally reaching the lofty status of chief financial officer of companies. I then made the mistake of starting my own business consulting company, and guess what? You guessed it…I had to SELL to get clients, which of course meant cold-calling prospective clients. I had a few clients that I had from previous associations, but then a miraculous thing happened…the 2008/09 financial collapse. Due to the nature of my client list being predominantly small businesses, I lost all but 2 of my clients.

During one of my periods while being an accountant I got involved with a community theater group, as an actor. I performed nine shows with them, and it brought me back into the 'artistic' mode of my early life in high school. I did *The Merchant of Venice, Wait Until Dark*, and seven others before I moved from the city to take a promotion. But the artistic side reared its ugly head, and I figured I wanted to do something in that vein.

With the advent of computers, I have found it fairly easy to begin writing projects. The idea for "Conversations with Myself" came to me as I was playing golf with some good friends. I am a particularly bad golfer, and I could get better if I were to practice, but that is something that I do not want to do right now. As I was playing, I hit a terrible slice (for you none-golfers, that is a ball that curves to the right if you are a right-handed golfer, which I am). I stood there, watching the ball go WAY right, and I said to myself, out loud, "Michael, what in the heck are you doing?"

What I did not realize is that I immediately answered by saying, out loud, "That is what you normally do. You have a habitual slice."

I then realized that over the course of years that I have lived on this earth, I have literally talked to myself at various times, and in various moods. So, I thought to myself, "what if I humanized those discussions by giving them names, and making a conversation between all of the various aspects of my personality"? I did, and I have had a great deal of fun and insight doing it. That is the origin of this treatise.

Coming up with the names and parts of my personality was simple, for the most part. The difficulty lay in making sense of what the feelings and thoughts were, and hopefully being consistent. I am not sure that I completely succeeded.

Here is a list of the 'personality' types and what they represent. In order to ensure that the reader does not get confused, I have given each of the personalities a different font that will contain what it is that they are saying. The fonts are listed below, after the small introduction to the character.

Mike is the basic person that most of us would meet and know. He is the persona that deals with the majority of all situations that I would deal with. FONT: **Rockwell Condensed**

MICHAEL is the version of me that I would suggest I am striving to be. His is the spiritual, reflective part that probably knows more about who and what we are. FONT: *ALGERIAN*

MIKEY is the side of my persona that flairs up in anger. He is what needs to be controlled or I would always be angry. FONT: **Arial Black**

WUM is my humorous side, or the me that always attempts to look at things from the humorous side. FONT: Kristen ITC

Dr. Mike is that aspect of my life that is known as the record keeper – the keeper of facts and statistics that we use from time to time. FONT: Ink Free

mr.mike is that aspect of my personality that sometimes exhibits the negative sides of my nature. I hope it does not rear its head very often. FONT: *Segoe Script*

MICKY is the part of my nature that has the deep, dark secrets. Once again, I hope it does not happen too often. FONT: **Broadway**

I have taken great pains to make sure that this is easy to read by having what each part of my personality says by a different type style. I chose to do this as I felt it would lend more difference or personality to each of the identities. The alternative was to put the name of the entity that was talking to the side, like a play. I chose not to do that so that the flow would be easier to follow, especially if the reader wants to make up different voices for the personalities. If I ever get this into an audio book, I will do that.

Now that you have this introduction into my thought process, I hope you enjoy reading this little attempt at introspection, human nature, quirks of individuals, anger, and humor.

My appreciation goes out to my wife's cousin, Maggi Neff; a very good friend and retired teacher, Kathy Shaw; and finally to my sister, Charlene Simcox. They were helpful in reading the manuscript, and correcting any obvious spelling and grammatical errors, and in general giving me feedback on the content. Thank you all for your help and positive input!

One last thing before you begin reading my little book. I do not believe that I am crazy, insane, or any other incantation used to describe the differences that we human beings are to one another.

Nor do I believe that any psychologist or psychiatrist would label me as such if they were to talk to me for more than three minutes. I just believe this exercise is simply my way of finding a way to express what we as human beings deal with on a daily basis, hopefully finding humor in most everything we do or say, some of it even being intentional. All of the thoughts, ideas. discussions, and writings are mine alone, and I am solely responsible for the content of this book.

I hope you will enjoy the trip.

Michael William Peterson
La Verne, CA
October 7, 2019

Road Rage

(Or driving would be easy if everyone were as good a driver as me)

Author's Note: Have you ever driven on the LA Freeways at rush hour? Sometimes the experiences can be very frightening, even when it is not rush hour. Inherently, we as human beings do not believe that we are EVER at fault or driving less than perfectly. It is always the other person's inadequacy that causes us to get just a tad angry while driving. Hence the following discussion…

Michael William Peterson

MIKEY...

WHAT!!!!!!!!!

MIKEY, WHAT IS THE PROBLEM?

DID YOU SEE WHAT THAT MORON DID? HE CUT RIGHT IN FRONT OF ME! HE ALMOST CAUSED AN ACCIDENT. JERK! WHERE DID YOU GET YOUR LICENSE - A COUPON BOOK FROM THE BRAILLE INSTITUTE?

MIKEY, CALMATE. THAT IS SPANISH BY THE WAY...

I KNOW THAT! I SPEAK SPANISH, YOU IDIOT. LOOK AT THIS CREEP...IF YOU ARE GOING TO DRIVE BENEATH THE SPEED LIMIT, PARK THE DAMN CAR AND GET A BIKE!

ARE YOU UPSET? YOU SEEM TO BE VERY ANGRY. EVERYTHING OKAY?

I JUST DO NOT UNDERSTAND HOW SOME PEOPLE DRIVE. IT DRIVES ME CRAZY...

NICE PUN...

AND CAUSES ACCIDENTS! AAAAAAAAGGGGGHHHHHHHHH!!!

CALMATE, MI HIJO. BREATHE DEEPLY...THAT'S A GOOD BOY... JUST FEEL THE SERENITY COMPLETELY OVERCOMING ANY ANGRY THOUGHTS INVADING YOUR SPACE...

2

Jerk. I tell ya...driving a car is frustrating, especially here where no one seems to know how to drive...the other day I almost got hit by a 'left turn artist' as I was trying to get through a yellow light...

FEEL THE PEACE AND QUIET...ALMOST AS GOOD AS LISTENING TO BACH OR MOZART...

Personally, I relax to the Beach Boys, Dave Brubeck, Lionel Hampton, or Peter Paul and Mary.

THAT IS A BIT OF AN ECLECTIC COLLECTION. ARE YOU A MUSIC FAN, MIKE?

Yes, I am. Most kinds, except rap or hip hop or whatever they are calling it these days. By the by, who are you?

DON'T YOU KNOW?

IF I KNEW, I PROBABLY WOULD NOT ASK, DON'T YOU THINK?

MIKEY...

WHAT?!

DO I NEED TO ASK YOU TO CALM DOWN AGAIN? IT ISN'T DOING YOUR BLOOD PRESSURE OR YOUR SELF ESTEEM ANY GOOD...

WHAT ARE YOU, MY PSYCHIATRIST?

DO YOU NEED ONE?

NO! WHO THE HECK ARE YOU?

I WILL TELL YOU, IF YOU WILL CALM DOWN. THAT'S IT... PAINTINGS BY RENOIR, KINCADE...

Picasso is more to my taste...

REALLY?

Yup. What is interesting in Picasso is that you can ultimately decide what it is exactly that you see in his paintings. The others you mention are fairly basic. Resplendent, but basic.

I SEE. MIKE, WHY DO YOU GET SO ANGRY WHEN YOU DRIVE?

I don't know...I wonder sometimes after I get angry just 'what WAS I thinking.'

IT DOESN'T HAPPEN VERY OFTEN, BUT IT HAPPENS A LOT MORE WHEN YOU DRIVE. DOES THAT SEEM TO BE CORRECT?

I would say that it doesn't happen very often at all...

THAT IS CORRECT. BUT IT DOES HAPPEN A LOT MORE OFTEN WHEN YOU ARE BEHIND THE WHEEL AND IN TRAFFIC. I HAVE NOTICED THAT WHEN YOU ARE DRIVING THROUGH A WILDERNESS AREA, FOR EXAMPLE, YOU VERY RARELY GET ANGRY.

Duh...there aren't THAT many idiots behind the wheel in the wilderness...

MAYBE IT IS THE TRAFFIC, THEN...I MEAN THINK ABOUT IT... DRIVING, LISTENING TO THE BEACH BOYS, GOING AS FAST AS YOU WANT, WITHIN LIMITS OF COURSE, AND NO ONE AROUND TO CUT IN FRONT OF YOU...PRETTY CLOSE TO HEAVEN AS NEAR AS I CAN TELL.

Yes, that would be nice. I know that I have asked you before, and you told me that you would tell me if I calmed down. Well, I am calm now, so, who are you?

YOU EVER READ PLATO?

Yes.

PLATO, IF MEMORY SERVES, SUGGESTS THAT THERE ARE THREE LEVELS OF REALITY – THE REAL, THE UNREAL, AND THE REALLY REAL. THE REALLY REAL IS WHAT I AM IF PLATO WERE TO LOOK AT YOU.

Excuse me?

I AM WHAT PLATO WOULD SUGGEST IS THE 'IDEAL'. I AM WHAT YOU WOULD BE IF YOU WERE THE BEST SELF THAT YOU COULD BE.

You are me?

YES. I AM YOU, AND YOU ARE ME. I AM JUST A DIFFERENT FACET OF YOUR EXISTENCE.

I see.

PEOPLE ARE REALLY A COMPLEX SET OF INDIVIDUALS WHO REACT TO DIFFERENT STIMULI AND DIFFERENT SITUATIONS, AND DEFENSIVELY DEAL WITH EACH STIMULI/SITUATION BY BRINGING OUT DIFFERENT FACETS OF THEIR PERSONALITIES.

But you are not real.

IN THE EXISTENTIAL SENSE OF THE WORD, WHAT IS "REAL"?

I can't see you...

JUST BECAUSE YOU CANNOT SEE SOMETHING DOES NOT NECESSARILY MEAN THAT IT DOES NOT EXIST OR IS NOT THERE. LOOK AT AIR FOR EXAMPLE – YOU CAN'T SEE IT, BUT IT IS THERE, THANK HEAVEN.

I can see the air in Los Angeles. Not as well as I used to, but I can still see it.

TRUE ENOUGH. POINT TAKEN. IF YOU WANT TO SEE ME, JUST LOOK IN A MIRROR.

I suppose that if what you say is true, then I guess I would see you.

EXCUSE ME – DID YOU SAY "IF"?

Ooops.

I SHOULD HOPE SO, MY FINE, FAT LITTLE FRIEND.

I am talking to you?

YES.

Isn't one of the signs of a crazy person is that they converse with themselves?

ONLY IF YOU ANSWER...

That is what conversing is...answering when another person asks or says something that requires a response.

JUST KIDDING. YOU REALLY NEED TO LIGHTEN UP. YOU ARE ENTIRELY TOO TENSE. HAVE YOU HAD SEX LATELY?

Pardon me?

HAVE YOU HAD SEX LATELY? IT IS A FAIR QUESTION. SEX ALWAYS HELP YOU RELAX. I KNOW IT HELPS ME RELAX.

Wouldn't you know if I have had sex recently?

YOU ARE FORGETTING ONE OF THE MAIN PREMISES OF THIS ARRANGEMENT. I HELP YOU WITH THINGS THAT ARE NOT QUITE OBVIOUS TO YOU IN YOUR DAILY ROUTINE. I AM MERELY ASKING YOU THE QUESTION SO THAT YOU ARE AWARE OF YOUR NEEDS, IN ALL AREAS, I MIGHT ADD.

So, basically, I am having a conversation with myself, and the topics of conversation will range all over the map.

THAT IS CORRECT.

And you do not think that makes me 'crazy'?

LET ME ASK YOU A QUESTION. IF YOU GO THROUGH THE PROCESS OF SELF-AWARENESS, BY THIS I MEAN THE PROCESS OF GETTING TO KNOW ONESELF BY ASKING DIFFICULT QUESTIONS WHEN TRYING TO IMPROVE ONE'S LIFE BY CHANGING THAT WHICH IS WRONG, DOES THAT MAKE YOU CRAZY?

No. But I am not trying to converse with myself either...

IF YOU DON'T VERBALIZE BUT YOU THINK THE QUESTION, WHAT IS THE DIFFERENCE? BESIDES, WHO WOULD YOU RATHER TALK WITH – SOMEONE WHO KNOWS YOU BETTER THAN YOU KNOW YOURSELF, ME, OR SOMEONE WHO DOES NOT HAVE A CLUE AS TO WHO YOU ARE AND WHAT YOU THINK?

I suppose...someone who knows me...so, I am not crazy because I am talking to myself?

IF I WERE TO SAY THAT YOU ARE CRAZY, THAT WOULD IMPLY THAT I AM CRAZY, WOULD IT NOT? AND, TO ANSWER THE QUESTION EVEN FURTHER, I AM NOT CRAZY. I MAY BE INTO DENIAL, BUT I AM NOT CRAZY. DON'T YOU REMEMBER WHEN YOU USED TO ASK YOURSELF QUESTIONS AND THEN YOUR MIND WOULD THEN RESPOND AND GIVE YOU AN ANSWER?

Yes...

THAT WAS ME. I AM JUST TAKING A SLIGHTLY MORE DIRECT APPROACH TO GIVING YOU YOUR ANSWERS THAN I USED TO.

So why did you suddenly decide to make yourself more, let's say, "direct"?

ROAD RAGE.

Excuse me?

ROAD RAGE. OVER THE LAST TWO OR THREE MONTHS I HAVE NOTICED THAT YOU HAVE BECOME MORE PRONE TO GETTING ANGRY WHEN YOU DRIVE, AND YOU BECOME A DIFFERENT PERSON. THAT PERSON I CALL MIKEY BECAUSE HE IS LIKE A LITTLE BOY WHO GETS VERY ANGRY WHEN SOMEONE DOES SOMETHING VERY MINOR THAT HE DOES NOT LIKE. I THINK WE CAN SAFELY ASSUME THAT IT IS OUR BEST INTEREST TO KEEP MIKEY UNDER CONTROL. HENCE, THAT IS WHY I HAVE COME OUT OF THE CLOSET, SO TO SPEAK.

Does it happen very often?

NO, IT DOES NOT.

Does Mikey know about you/us?

YES, BUT HE SHEEPISHLY TRIES TO IGNORE US. USUALLY, HE IS NOT A RATIONAL BEING, SO HE DOES NOT REALLY WANT TO LISTEN TO US. MIKEY IS A BIT OF A TWIT.

Nice rhyme. May I ask you a question?

CERTAINLY. YOU JUST DID.

I know. You are a bit of a smart aleck, aren't you?

I AM WHAT YOU SHOULD BE, BUT NO ONE IS PERFECT.

I get the feeling that you are going to be talking to me quite a bit...

PROBABLY.

Is it your goal in life to irritate me?

NO, JUST ONE OF LIFE'S PLEASURES. JUST THINK OF IT AS AN OPPORTUNITY TO HAVE A GUIDE TO BEING A BETTER PERSON. I WANT YOU TO BE THE BEST POSSIBLE MIKE PETERSON THAT YOU CAN BE – ME.

Rather sure of yourself aren't you?

YES, I AM.

Well, so be it. Guess I am stuck with you.

YES, THAT IS CORRECT.

Well, to paraphrase you 'I guess there is no one that I would rather talk to than myself.'

COULD NOT HAVE SAID IT BETTER MYSELF.

You did.

(or "Wickedness never was happiness" and
other unbelievable platitudes)

Author's Note: Sometimes we just need a little time to relax and enjoy ourselves. This morning I was taking the time to reflect a little on my own status in the "Pursuit of Happiness". Sometimes we can relax with others, sometimes by ourselves, sometimes with others within ourselves.

GOOD MORNING, MIKE. HOW ARE YOU TODAY?

Okay, I guess. Just sitting down to read the paper. I love Sunday mornings. A time to relax, eat a leisurely breakfast, read the paper, get ready for church...all in all a pretty darn good day.

ARE YOU HAPPY?

What?

ARE YOU HAPPY?

What does that mean?

WHICH OF THESE THREE WORDS DO YOU NOT RECOGNIZE OR UNDERSTAND?

I understand all of them, but it is a rather complex question.

I KNOW. WHY DO YOU THINK I ASKED YOU?

Are you happy?

I WOULD BE IF YOU WERE A BETTER PERSON.

Excuse me?

IF I AM THE IDEAL MIKE PETERSON, THEN I SHOULD BE HAPPY BECAUSE I AM THE BEST THAT I CAN POSSIBLY BE. BUT I SUPPOSE AS LONG AS YOU ARE LESS THAN IDEAL, THEN I AM NOT HAPPY BECAUSE YOU ARE NOT THE BEST YOU CAN BE. "BE ALL YOU CAN BE, IN THE AAAAARMY!" I ALWAYS HATED THAT SONG.

So, you are not happy as long as I am not the best person that I can possibly be.

I AM NOT SURE THAT IS A TOTALLY ACCURATE STATEMENT.

Why?

BECAUSE THAT WOULD NECESSITATE YOU ALWAYS BEING ME IN ORDER FOR ME TO BE HAPPY, AND THAT WOULD ALSO SUGGEST THAT I AM NOT HAPPY WHEN YOU ARE NOT ME. BUT SINCE YOU ARE ALWAYS ME ANYWAY HOW CAN I BE HAPPY WHEN YOU ARE NOT, OR UNHAPPY WHEN YOU ARE NOT, OR VICE-VERSA.

I don't think I quite understood that, but that is okay...

IT REALLY IS QUITE SIMPLE. TO PUT IT IN A WAY THAT HOPEFULLY WILL EXPLAIN IT, LET'S TALK ABOUT BASKETBALL. DO YOU LIKE TO PLAY BASKETBALL?

Of course. You know that.

ARE YOU HAPPY WHEN YOU ARE PLAYING BASKETBALL?

I am not sure that 'happy' is a term that can be associated with playing basketball. I enjoy it immensely.

OKAY, YOU ENJOY IT IMMENSELY. DO YOU WIN WHEN YOU PLAY?

Sometimes. When we play well, I suppose.

ARE YOU HAPPY WHEN YOU WIN?

Sure.

SO, THERE CAN BE 'HAPPINESS' ATTAINED FROM BASKETBALL.

13

Yes, you made your point. I admit it, one can be happy playing basketball.

WHAT IF YOU PLAYED AGAINST THE LOS ANGELES LAKERS, YOU DID THE BEST THAT YOU COULD, AND THEY WON...

As if!

...WOULD YOU STILL BE HAPPY?

If I were good enough to play against the Lakers, that would mean that I am good enough to play in the NBA, correct? I mean, let's face it, the Lakers aren't going to have a scrimmage against my church team...

THAT IS NOT THE POINT...

It most certainly is the point. Because if I were in the NBA, you and I probably would not be having this conversation. I would be making, oh, easily a million per year in salary, and another million per year in endorsements playing the greatest game that was ever invented. I would be making about twenty times what I am making now doing what I love most. Well, second most, at any rate. Then, would that not define "happiness"?

I SEE YOUR POINT, BUT REALLY A PERSON CAN BE 'HAPPY' IF THEY WIN OR LOSE DEPENDING ON OTHER FACTORS. IF YOU DO YOUR BEST, AND STILL LOSE, SHOULD YOU NOT STILL BE HAPPY?

Yes, that is why we have the Los Angeles Clippers. But there is a danger in saying that. If you are content and happy just playing and not winning, you may not be in the league very long. At that level, winning is everything.

THERE IS A DIFFERENCE BETWEEN BEING CONTENT AND HAPPY.

Aren't they related?

YES, BUT THEY ARE NOT IDENTICAL.

Okay, show me a person who is content, but not happy, or vice-versa.

YOU.

That is a matter of opinion or argument. Besides, I am not sure that it is correct.

How about Mikey?

I would suggest that Mikey is not happy because by the very definition of angry, mean, spiteful, you cannot be happy.

IS HE CONTENT?

Probably.

HOLD ON A MINUTE. WHY AM I THE ONE YOU GUYS ALWAYS TALK ABOUT WHEN IT IS INTENSE NEGATIVITY THAT YOU DISCUSS?

GOOD MORNING, MIKEY. NICE OF YOU TO JOIN US.

YOU ARE AN IDIOT.

WHO ARE YOU TALKING TO?

YOU, DIPSTICK.

GO MIKEY!

WHO ARE YOU?

Who are you?

WHO THE HECK ARE YOU?

15

JUST ANOTHER BEING IN THIS HAPPY LITTLE FAMILY! YOU CAN CALL ME 'WUM'.

OH BOY, I KNOW YOU.

YES, YOU DO.

WHAT KIND OF STUPID, IGNORANT NAME IS WUM?

IT IS OUR MIDDLE NAME.

NO, OUR MIDDLE NAME IS WILLIAM.

NO, IT IS WUM.

I AM STAYING OUT OF THIS...

SMART MOVE, 'MISTER IDEAL'.

I believe that Mikey is right. Our middle name is William, named after our Grandfather, William, on our mother's side.

YES, THAT IS WHAT WAS INTENDED, BUT IF YOU CAREFULLY CHECK THE BIRTH CERTIFICATE, YOU WILL FIND THE MIDDLE NAME IS "WM".

Yes, and Wm is an abbreviation for William.

IF THERE WERE A PERIOD ("."") AFTER THE 'WM', I WOULD AGREE. BUT THERE IS NOT. THEREFORE, THE MIDDLE NAME IS 'WM', AND I DON'T KNOW TOO MANY OTHER WAYS OF PRONOUNCING 'WM' THAN WUM.

MIKE AND MIKEY, THIS PERSON IS NOT QUITE PLAYING WITH A FULL DECK...

OH, BE QUIET, MICHAEL. YOU DON'T LIKE ME 'CUZ I LIKE TO MAKE FUN OF YOU. GUYS, I AM THE HUMOROUS SIDE OF THE FAMILY, AND IT IS MY JOB TO NOT LET ANY OF YOU TAKE YOURSELVES TOO SERIOUSLY. BELIEVE ME, IT IS QUITE A JOB AT TIMES.

I can live with that. We were just discussing happiness...

YES, I KNOW. I WAS THERE. I WAS JUST LISTENING, FEASTING UPON MICHAEL'S BRILLIANT METAPHOR!

IT WAS A GOOD ONE...

If you two can't be civil to each other, Mikey and I will have this conversation alone.

Mikey, can you truly be happy being mean and nasty to everyone?

I AM NOT MEAN AND NASTY TO EVERYONE, ONLY TO THOSE MORONS WHO DESERVE IT.

And who deserves it?

ANYONE WHO DOES SOMETHING THAT (1.) I DON'T LIKE; OR (2.) IS STUPID; OR (3.) ANY COMBINATION OF THE FIRST TWO.

Okay, but why get angry with them?

BECAUSE, MISTER 'TRY TO BE NICE TO EVERYONE', IT LETS THEM KNOW THAT THEY ARE CAUSING OTHER PEOPLE PROBLEMS! PEOPLE SHOULD NOT GO AROUND CAUSING OTHER PEOPLE PROBLEMS!

YO, MIKEY, AREN'T YOU DOING THE SAME THING TO THEM?

IT'S DIFFERENT...

HOW?

THEY ARE CAUSING ME A PROBLEM! WHY SHOULD I HAVE TO PAY FOR THEIR STUPIDITY? THEY SHOULD BE HELD ACCOUNTABLE AND RESPONSIBLE FOR THEIR STUPID ACTS.

And you are holding them accountable and responsible by being angry at them?

GEE WHIZ. IT MUST BE TOUGH BEING THE ARBITRATOR AND SHERIFF FOR THE WHOLE WORLD! I ENVY YOUR PATIENCE FOR LIVING IN SUCH AN IMPERFECT WORLD, WITH SUCH IMPERFECT MORTALS!

SHUT UP, FUNNYMAN!

Mikey, all he is trying to do is to point out to you that you may be causing your own problems.

MY PROBLEM IS PRECISELY THAT I LIVE IN AN IMPERFECT WORLD.

MIKEY, IT SOUNDS TO ME AS IF YOU ARE ALLOWING OTHER PEOPLE AND THEIR ACTIONS DICTATE TO YOU HOW YOU ARE GOING TO ACT. THAT WOULD MEAN THAT YOU ARE ALLOWING OTHER PEOPLE TO CONTROL YOU BECAUSE YOU REACT TO THEIR ACTIONS INSTEAD OF ACTING THE WAY YOU DESIRE AND WANT TO.

I THINK HE HAS A POINT THERE, MIKEY.

Yes, I think he does.

IF THAT IS THE CASE, THEN WHAT SHOULD I DO WHEN SOME MORON CAUSES AN ACCIDENT AND I SUFFER?

SUE THE JERK! THAT WILL TEACH HIM RESPONSIBILITY AND ACCOUNTABILITY...

Yes, and you will get something from that...maybe a new car. I would like a new car...

THAT IS BESIDE THE POINT. WE ARE TALKING ABOUT BEING IN CONTROL OF YOURSELF, BEING THE BEST PERSON THAT YOU CAN BE, AND THAT YOU CAN CONTROL YOUR ANGER. BY DOING SO YOU WILL CONTROL YOUR THOUGHTS AND ACTIONS, AND NOT LET OTHER PEOPLE CONTROL YOU. REMEMBER WHAT DAD TOLD YOU ABOUT YOUR BROTHER JON KNOWING HOW TO CONTROL YOU. BUT, THE MOST IMPORTANT THING IS THAT YOU WILL BE IN CONTROL OF YOURSELF.

Yes, I remember that. What a great lesson and teaching moment! And Jon never really tried to control me after that.

HE WAS A FANTASTIC BIG BROTHER AFTER THAT! STILL IS, EVEN THOUGH HE HAS PASSED ON.

I wish I could see him again.

YOU WILL.

HELLO!!!!!! CAN WE GET BACK TO THE SUBJECT AT HAND? THANK YOU! I KNOW I USED TO CONTROL MYSELF, AND I AM TRYING. BUT WHAT IF SOMEONE DOES SOMETHING I DON'T LIKE,

BUT COULD HAVE CAUSED HARM? CAN'T I GET ANGRY THEN?

WHAT GOOD WOULD IT DO? NOTHING OR NO ONE WAS HURT, AND MAYBE THE PERSON WAS NOT INTENTIONALLY OUT TO HURT YOU. HAVE YOU EVER DONE THAT?

I SUPPOSE.

VERY WELL, DID YOU ENJOY THE OTHER PERSON YELLING AND SCREAMING AND CALLING YOU "MORON".

NOT REALLY.

THAT KIND OF BEHAVIOR REALLY IS IDIOTIC, ISN'T IT?

IT REALLY ONLY HURTS YOURSELF WHEN THINGS LIKE THAT HAPPEN.

There are a ton of people in this world who act like that. Just walking around, angry, waiting for someone to do something ever so slightly different and then they can justify their anger.

DO YOU THINK THEY ARE HAPPY?

NO, BUT THEY MAY BE CONTENT!

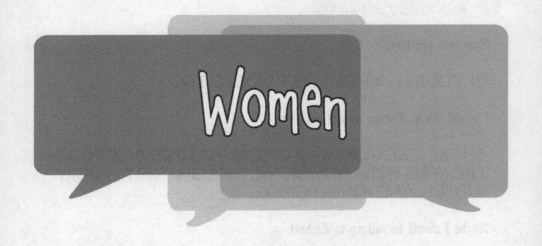

Women

(or "One of Nature's More Agreeable Blunders", Mark Twain)

Author's Note: There are times in our lives when we just have to throw up our hands because we do not understand or comprehend what is going on. A lot of time this lack of understanding or comprehension has to do with the members of the opposite sex, in my case, women. I skipped a grade and, as a result, was probably the youngest in my class, and this probably did not help my prowess in understanding the opposite sex when puberty hit, and then probably became worse when the dating process began in high school where I dated mostly young ladies that were older than myself. As a result, the following dialogue is not only appropriate, but probably very real and accurate, and true. Enjoy/

Wum, are you there?

OF COURSE, WHERE ELSE WOULD I BE?

I would like to discuss women with you.

AH YES. CERTAINLY, A TOPIC THAT DESERVES TO BE TREATED WITH HUMOR, ALTHOUGH, BE IT A VERY SUBTLE, AND KIND, HUMOR.

Maybe I should be talking to Michael.

I AM HERE. WHAT IS THE PROBLEM WITH WOMEN?

No problem, just wanted to discuss them with you.

OKAY. IN ORDER TO DO SO, WE SHOULD BASICALLY SET UP SOME GROUND RULES, AND CLARIFY SOME BASIC ASSUMPTIONS.

Why? I just want to talk about them, not categorize and date them...

YOU DON'T WANT TO DATE WOMEN? ARE WE GAY?

No, I am not gay. What I meant was, I would like to have a generalized discussion about them...

YES, AND IN ORDER TO PROCEED THERE MAY BE SOME THINGS THAT ARE NEEDED TO BE AGREED UPON. SUCH AS, THE REASON WHY THEY ARE DIFFERENT FROM US, WHAT CAN AND SHOULD BE SAID ABOUT THEM...

Guys, don't read too much into this. I just want to talk about women...

AND, IT WOULD HELP ME TO UNDERSTAND YOUR QUESTIONS IF WE SETTLED ON SOME BASIC COMMON GROUND...

WHAT COMMON GROUND? WE ARE THE SAME PERSON! AIN'T ANY MORE COMMON GROUND THAN THAT!

DO YOU HAVE TO BE HERE?

AS LONG AS I HAVE TO BE, YES.

DON QUIJOTE HAD HIS SANCHO PANZA, I GUESS YOU WILL HAVE TO BE MY WUM.

FINALLY, YOU RECOGNIZE OUR GENIUS!

Excuse me, but do I have to be here for this?

SORRY...

SORRY.

WHERE WERE WE? OH YES. WOMEN.

Rules and Assumptions...

WE MUST PROCEED, FOR OUR PURPOSES, ON THE FOLLOWING ASSUMPTIONS. ONE, THE FEMALE (WOMAN) OF THE SPECIES IS DIFFERENT FROM THE MALE (MAN) OF THE SPECIES IN SEVERAL RESPECTS. TWO, THE NATURE OF THESE DIFFERENCES SUGGESTS SOME OF THE ATTRIBUTES WITHIN THE GENDER. THREE, THESE ATTRIBUTES OCCUR MORE NATURALLY IN WOMAN, BUT CAN BE LEARNED BY MEN, IF THEY APPLY THEMSELVES. FOUR...

All I want to do is talk about women, for crying out loud. I just want to ask some basic questions.

I KNOW THAT, BUT I AM JUST GIVING YOU A FORMAT FROM WHICH TO PROCEED.

I do not want a format. I just want to discuss women. Maybe I should ask Mikey...I am sure he can discuss this without a format...

NO. HE IS BETTER OFF OUT OF THIS ONE! TRUST ME.

I AGREE WITH WUM.

THANK YOU, MICHAEL.

YOU ARE WELCOME...

Are you guys finished? Now, I am not quite sure that I understand women.

DON'T WORRY ABOUT IT. NEITHER DOES ANY OTHER MAN. OR FOR THAT MATTER, NEITHER DOES ANY OTHER WOMAN.

MY FRIEND HERE IS QUITE CORRECT. THE COMPLEXITIES OF ANY HUMAN BEING ARE SUCH THAT TO UNDERSTAND THEM WOULD TAKE A LIFETIME OF STUDY. IF YOU WANT TO SUGGEST THAT YOU WOULD LIKE TO UNDERSTAND ONE WOMAN, FOR EXAMPLE, OUR BEAUTIFUL AND MAGNIFICENT PATTI, THEN THAT IS POSSIBLE, AND A DELIGHTFUL ENTERPRISE. TO ATTEMPT TO UNDERSTAND MORE THAN ONE, HOWEVER, IS FRAUGHT WITH PERIL.

Why?

BECAUSE OF THE NATURE OF HUMAN RELATIONS, MY DEAR MIKE. WE HUMAN BEINGS ARE SEVERELY LIMITED IN OUR ABILITY TO RELATE TO MORE THAN ONE HUMAN BEING AT A TIME BECAUSE WE DO NOT POSSESS THE OUTWARD AWARENESS TO DO IT. ESPECIALLY MEN. MEN CAN RELATE, ON A VERY PRIMAL LEVEL, TO AS MANY OF THE OPPOSITE SEX AS HE DESIRES BUT THAT IS NOT A MEANS OF UNDERSTANDING THEM.

Are we talking about sex?

ONLY AS IT GETS IN THE WAY OF UNDERSTANDING WOMEN. MEN MAKE THE MISTAKE OF EQUATING SEX WITH ROMANCE, LOVE WITH SEX, AND THE MORE WOMEN WITH WHICH YOU HAVE SEX THE MORE YOU UNDERSTAND WOMEN...

MEN, THEY ARE SUCH PIGS.

...AND THAT IS A MISTAKE OF HUGE PROPORTIONS.

Oh. So, what you are truly saying, if I understand you correctly, is that if I want to understand women, it is best to study and understand one, rather than try to understand many.

THAT IS CORRECT. TO UNDERSTAND ONE WOMAN, YOU NEED TO BE WITH AND THINK AND TALK WITH SAID PERSON FOR LONG TIME BECAUSE OF THEIR COMPLEXITY, AND THERE IS VERY LITTLE TIME FOR MOST MEN TO BE ABLE TO DO THAT WITH ANYONE BUT ONE WOMAN, USUALLY HIS WIFE.

Generally speaking, then, you would make the leap to suggest that all women are the same.

IN TERMS OF THE GENERAL ATTRIBUTES, YES, I BELIEVE THEY ARE.

Can't you say the same thing about men?

YES, EVEN MORE SO. MEN TEND TO FALL INTO A MUCH SMALLER CLASSIFICATION OF DIFFERENCES THAN WOMEN. BY THAT I MEAN THAT MEN ARE MORE AKIN TO THEIR GENDER NORM THAN WOMEN ARE...

If you were to look at it statistically, it would probably mean that the mean standard deviation of men is plus or minus .3%, while the mean standard deviation of women would be plus or minus 3.19%.

Who are you?

I do not have a name.

What is your function in our person?

HE IS THE MAN WITH THE NUMBERS. HE ONLY DEALS IN FACTS, SOMETHING THAT CAN BE PUT IN A MATHEMATICAL EQUATION. WE DON'T LET HIM OUT VERY OFTEN...

Nor, quite frankly do I wish to come out very often. I am much more comfortable at home with my numbers than I am dealing with people, especially those people who like to generalize without any real basis of fact behind them. Therefore, most people have no idea of what they are really talking about, and I just stay out of the conversations rather than embarrassing them. It is one of those things that literally drives me up a wall, so I do not socialize very much.

I see. So, you are the guy with the facts and figures, so to speak,

Yes.

But how do I know that your facts are correct?

I beg your pardon?

How do I know that what you are telling me, or the figures that you came up with, are correct?

As long as you use them, it won't matter. Let me give you an example. What did I say about the mean standard deviation of men and women?

26

Basically, that men fit the pattern of male-ness, for want of a better term, than women do of women-ness, by the lower mean standard deviation. For men it was plus or minus .3%, and for women it was plus or minus 3.19%.

That is correct. Where did I get those figures?

I assume that you got them from some study...

Mike, Mike, Mike, Mike, Mike...

What, what, what, what, what?

Do you really think there is a study which would measure that sort of thing? How, in Heaven's name, would you have the audacity to even attempt to decide what is normal "male-ness"?

I am not sure I understand what you are saying...

Just because I quote a number does not necessarily mean that it is really correct, or even real.

You make things up?

People do it all the time. Have you ever watched a Presidential debate? Besides, one of the books we read in college was entitled "How to Lie with Statistics". Do you remember that?

Yes, but the author wasn't talking about making up things as you go along.

I THINK I NEED TO STEP IN HERE FOR A MOMENT. MIKE, THIS IS DR. MIKE AND HE IS NOT TALKING ABOUT ALWAYS MAKING THINGS UP. HE IS YOUR LIBRARIAN OF BASIC INFORMATION THAT MOST PEOPLE WOULD FIND TRIVIAL AND DULL, BUT THAT HE FINDS FASCINATING. THERE IS A PART OF EVERY HUMAN THAT LIKES KNOWING USELESS TRIVIA

SIMPLY BECAUSE NO ONE ELSE KNOWS IT OR KNOWS QUITE AS MUCH AS THE INDIVIDUAL LIKES TO THINK HE DOES. DR. MIKE IS YOUR KEEPER OF THAT PART OF YOUR PSYCHE, AND WELL, AS HE SAID, PEOPLE OFTEN LIKE TO MAKE THINGS UP BECAUSE TO QUOTE A NUMBER, OR A VAGUE OR UNKNOWN SOURCE, ALWAYS SOUNDS AUTHORITATIVE.

Thank you, Michael. That was very well put.

So, you don't really have any information about women, of a statistical nature, do you?

Yes, but not the kind that you are looking for. To quote a present-day euphemism 'there isn't any such animal!'

Meaning...

THERE IS NOT A BUNCH OF STATISTICS THAT ARE GOING TO HELP YOU UNDERSTAND WOMEN...

Precisely.

Then, how am I going to understand them?

Like 99.9999999% of the men that try, you will never succeed. Men do not have the attribute of enough patience to understand women, so do yourself a favor and don't try. It will save yourself a lot of worry and heartache.

Why?

BECAUSE, MY DEAR MIKE, JUST WHEN YOU THINK YOU UNDERSTAND THEM, THEY CHANGE THE RULES, THINGS ARE DIFFERENT, AND 'VIOLA!', YOU ARE BACK TO SQUARE ONE.

Then you are saying that women understand men a lot better than men understand women, yes?

PRECISELY.

Then, they have an advantage and can control us?

CORRECT.

They can control us as much as they desire.

How do we, as men, fall for that?

IT IS BECAUSE OF OUR BASIC LACK OF UNDERSTANDING ABOUT THE 'NATURE OF THE BEAST', SO TO SPEAK.

You will find that the woman of the species is considerably more adept at controlling us than we are at controlling them. 70.1% of men think that they are in control, and it is because the woman allows him to think so.

NOT ME!

MIKEY, GO BACK TO SLEEP. THIS IS A SUBJECT UPON WHICH YOU CAN HAVE VERY LITTLE POSITIVE INPUT.

So, let me see if I understand this correctly. Generally, women, by their nature and disposition, understand men better than men understand women. Therefore, it is easier for them to manipulate and control us, and they do that by allowing us men to believe the myth of being 'Kings in our Castles' and that we control our universe. Is that a fair assumption?

YES, IT IS.

I believe that is correct.

Wow. That is the pits.

NOT NECESSARILY. IF WE UNDERSTAND THAT WE DO NOT UNDERSTAND THEM, AND ACT ACCORDINGLY, KNOWING THAT THEY ARE MANIPULATING US, THEN WE DO UNDERSTAND THEM, AND IT THEN BECOMES EASIER TO LIVE WITH THEIR IDIOSYNCRASIES AND ILLOGICAL BEHAVIOR.

So, we do understand them...

AS MUCH AS WE CAN, AND IF YOU CAN CALL IT UNDERSTANDING. REMEMBER KING ARTHUR IN "*CAMELOT*" AND THE SONG "*HOW TO HANDLE A WOMAN*"? ARTHUR SAYS MERLIN ONCE SAID 'NEVER BE CONCERNED WHEN A WOMAN IS THINKING...THEY DON'T DO IT VERY OFTEN".

CUTE, WUM, BUT NOT QUITE RIGHT. WE MEN UNDERSTAND THEM AS MUCH AS A WOMAN ALLOWS HERSELF TO BE UNDERSTOOD, AND BECAUSE OF THE DIFFERENCES, WE MEN WILL GRASP AND HOLD ON TO IT BECAUSE WE DO RECOGNIZE THAT, IN THE WHOLE OF GOD'S WONDERFUL CREATIONS, WOMAN IS HIS CROWNING ACHIEVEMENT, AND IS WHAT CAUSES MEN TO THE BEST THAT THEY CAN BE. TOGETHER, MAN AND WOMAN MAKE A FORMIDABLE PAIR, AND THE JOURNEY THROUGH LIFE CAN BE A JOURNEY OF GRAND AND EPIC PROPORTIONS. AFTER ALL, WHAT WOULD OUR LIFE BE WITHOUT OUR PATTI?

I am afraid that I would not want to experience that.

TO QUOTE THE COWARDLY LION IN THE 'WIZARD OF OZ'..."AIN'T IT THE TRUTH! AIN'T IT THE TRUTH

(One of the other necessary evils of this world)

Author's Note: Work. One of life's four-letter words. I have been working fairly regularly since my early years in high school. There are a lot of jobs that I really did not like, and there were some jobs that I really enjoyed. I literally worked for other people pretty much my whole career, and there were some bosses that I liked, and some I did not. The discussion below is very broad in order to capture the whole gamut of emotions that go into successful work, as well as unsuccessful work. I have experienced both.

MIKE...WAKE UP...IT IS TIME TO GET UP AND GO TO WORK.

I DON'T WANT TO.

MIKEY, GO BACK TO SLEEP. MIKE NEEDS TO GET UP AND GO TO WORK.

I don't want to...

YOU HAVE TO.

Why?

WE HAVE TO WORK SO THAT WE CAN EAT.

I am too fat anyway.

YES, WE ARE. BUT WE STILL NEED TO EAT. IF WE DO NOT EAT, WE DIE, AND I AM NOT SURE THAT PATTI WOULD APPRECIATE LIVING WITH A DEAD PERSON. GET UP!

I still do not want to. I do not want to go to that job today.

MIKE, I REALIZE THAT, BUT UNFORTUNATELY YOU HAVE RESPONSIBILITIES THAT REQUIRE YOU TO GO AND MAKE MONEY. YOU HAVE A HOUSE, CAR PAYMENTS, DEBTS, CHILDREN, AND YOU NEED TO GET UP AND GO TO WORK SO THAT YOU CAN SUPPORT ALL OF THOSE THINGS.

Now I am sure that I do not want to get up and go to work.

MIKE...

No. I am not going there today. I need sleep.

THEN GO TO BED EARLIER, YOU TWIT. STAYING UP UNTIL 1:00 AM JUST TO WATCH THE NEWS OR JERRY SPRINGER IS NOT CONDUCIVE TO OUR HEALTH.

No. I am not going. I hate that job. Too much stress...too many people yelling at me...too many vendors calling asking for money...it is driving me crazy.

BETTER YOU THAN US!

WUM, SHUT UP. JEEZ. MIKE, YOU HAVE A GREAT JOB WHEREIN YOU ARE PAID A LOT OF MONEY TO DO WHAT YOU DO, AND YOU ARE GOOD AT IT.

I want to work at McDonalds's. Maybe there is not quite so much pressure there...

YES, I AM SURE THAT YOU WOULD LIKE SLINGING HAMBURGERS AT YOUR AGE!

It could be worse...didn't you see *"American Beauty"* with Kevin Spacey? He did it, and he seemed to be happy...

YES, AND LOOK HOW HE ENDED UP.

That was not his fault. I could like flipping burgers for $12.75 an hour.

MIKE...

Let me try. Mike, you have a mortgage on your house that you have to pay for. It is approximately $2,678.53 per month. You have two nice cars that you drive (one at $537.19, the other at $448.79). You have other debt that you have incurred that costs you an additional $527.00 per month. You have household expenses, including groceries, of up to $1,578.00 per month. You pay $2.000 per month for you church and other charities. You have insurance policies, savings plan, mutual funds that take more of your income. In total. You spend about $10,000.00 per month. If you worked at McDonald's for $12.75 per hour, you would make a

33

total of $26, 265 for the whole year, when, after taxes, would not even pay your expenses for two months.

Okay, I get your point. I am getting up. Thank you for such an inspirational point of view, Dr. Mike.

You are welcome.

MIKE, ONE THING YOU HAVE TO UNDERSTAND IS THAT SARCASM IS LOST ON DR. MIKE. BUT HE DID GET THE POINT ACROSS, DID HE NOT?

Yes, he did.

THEN HE DOES SERVE A USEFUL PURPOSE, AS MOST ALL OF US DO.

DR. MIKE JUST DOESN'T HAVE A SENSE OF HUMOR. HE DRIVES ME CRAZY TOO.

Glad that I am not alone.

GOOD ONE!

It is just that I really haven't enjoyed my job for a long time.

THEN FIND A NEW ONE.

At my age?

YES, WE ARE NOT THAT OLD!

I am at the age when people should begin thinking about retiring, not switching jobs...

Excuse me, but I think we should have been thinking and planning for retirement a lot sooner than now.

YES, DR. MIKE, POINT WELL TAKEN. MIKE, YOU HAVE THE POWER TO CHANGE YOUR LIFE, AND ONLY YOU HAVE THAT POWER. IF YOU DO NOT LIKE YOUR SITUATION, THEN CHANGE IT. YOU CAN DO ANYTHING YOU WANT TO.

Can I play centerfield for the New York Yankees?

WITHIN REASON, YOU CAN DO ANYTHING YOU SET YOUR MIND TO DO. IF YOU WERE IN YOUR MID 20'S, YES I WOULD SAY THAT YOU COULD TRY FOR IT. BUT I DO NOT THINK THAT AT 60 THE YANKEES ARE GOING TO WANT TO GIVE A TRYOUT TO AN OUT OF SHAPE MAN WHOSE SKILLS HAVE DIMINISHED.

Gee, thanks for the encouragement.

THE POINT IS THAT YOU ARE A CAPABLE INDIVIDUAL THAT CAN DO MANY THINGS. YOU HAVE A GREAT DEAL OF EXPERIENCE. THERE ARE A GREAT MANY THINGS THAT YOU CAN DO. YOU JUST NEED TO DECIDE WHAT IT IS YOU WANT TO DO.

Can I start my own company?

DOING WHAT, MAY I ASK?

Accounting and financial consulting.

SURE. YOU ARE CERTAINLY EXPERIENCED AND CAPABLE. YOU DO NOT, HOWEVER, HAVE A CPA...

I know that.

SO, YOU COULD NOT START YOUR OWN CPA FIRM...

WHO WANTS TO DO THAT? I AM FIRMLY CONVINCED THAT ONLY GEEKS, DORKS, AND SUCH LIKE DR. MIKE WOULD WORK AS CPA'S!

Be kind, Wum. They serve a purpose. They make life miserable for the rest of us!

COME ON YOU GUYS. KNOCK IT OFF. CPA'S ARE GOOD PEOPLE. THEY PERFORM NECESSARY EVILS IN LIFE AS REQUIRED BY OUR TAX LAWS AND OUR SECURITIES LAWS.

I know. But one does not have to be a CPA to offer a service to companies and businesses. Could I teach?

YES. BUT YOU WILL HAVE TO TAKE A RATHER LARGE PAY CUT. TEACHERS UNFORTUNATELY GET PAID A LOT LESS THAN ACCOUNTANTS!

WUM IS RIGHT. IT WOULD BE A RATHER LARGE PAY CUT.

I AM NOT TAKING A PAYCUT! I JUST TOOK ONE OF THOSE AT WORK SO THAT THE BOSS' SON COULD CONTINUE HIS LIFESTYLE. I AIN'T DOING ANOTHER ONE!

Mikey, do not worry. That is a separate issue.

IS THAT ONE OF THE REASONS YOU ARE SO UNHAPPY AT WORK?

Well, let's just say that I have differences in how things should be run than my boss does.

HERE IS THE DEAL. IF YOU ARE UNHAPPY ENOUGH TO CHANGE IT, YOU WILL. IF NOT, THEN YOU WON'T. IT IS ENTIRELY YOUR DECISION. BUT YOU CAN DO ANYTHING YOU WANT TO. YOU ARE A VERY CAPABLE PERSON.

But, if I started my own company, how would I sell it? I am not a salesman.

THEREIN LIES THE PROBLEM OF ALL SMALL BUSINESSES, AND QUITE FRANKLY, MOST ACCOUNTING PROFESSIONALS.

IF YOU DECIDE TO DO IT, YOU WILL FIND A WAY. BESIDES, IT IS NOT THE SALES PROCESS YOU ARE AFRAID OF, IT IS THE MARKETING THAT YOU ARE CONCERNED ABOUT.

SAME DIFFERENCE!

NO, ACTUALLY IT IS NOT. MIKE, WHAT IS THE PART THAT YOU HATE ABOUT SELLING?

That is an easy question to answer. Calling on the phone for appointments.

YOU MEAN THAT ONCE YOU GET AN APPOINTMENT, YOU DO NOT MIND TALKING TO PEOPLE?

No, I do not mind that. I actually enjoy it.

IT IS THE COLD CALLING AND THE PROSPECTING AND THE FEAR OF REJECTION THAT COMES WITH COLD CALLING THAT YOU DO NOT LIKE. DO YOU FEEL REJECTED IF YOU TALK TO PEOPLE, IN PERSON, AND THEY DO NOT ACCEPT YOUR PROPOSAL?

No, because then I have the opportunity to discuss it with them, and I can probably convince them to accept the proposal as it is to their benefit.

SO, YOU CAN SELL YOUR IDEAS AS LONG AS IT IS NOT A COLD CALL OR ON THE PHONE?

Yes, I believe that I can.

THAT THEN IS AN OBSTACLE TO BE OVERCOME IN THE BUSINESS PLAN. CAN YOU OFFER A SERVICE THAT IS VALUABLE TO PEOPLE?

Valuable because it will save them money in the long run and make their businesses run more efficiently, yes.

THEN WHY NOT DO IT, MORON!

MIKEY, QUIET. THEN WHY NOT DO IT?

I don't know...

ARE YOU AFRAID?

Probably.

COULD YOU BE ANY MORE VAGUE IN YOUR ANSWER?

WUM, QUIET. WHAT ARE YOU AFRAID OF?

Failure. Being viewed as a stupid idea. The fear that I won't be able to make the money that I need, or that Dr. Mike says I need to live.

LET'S TALK ABOUT EACH OF THESE FEARS. DO YOU BELIEVE THAT THE IDEA YOU HAVE IS VALUABLE TO COMPANIES?

Yes.

DO YOU BELIEVE THAT IT CAN BE OF HELP TO BUSINESSES AND ORGANIZATIONS?

Yes.

DO YOU BELIEVE THERE IS A MARKET FOR THESE SERVICES?

Yes.

THEN, IT DOESN'T SEEM TO BE SUCH A STUPID IDEA, DOES IT?

SCORE ONE FOR THE GOOD GUYS!

But there is competition…

SO, IT IS MORE THE COMPETITION THAT YOU ARE AFRAID OF?

Well, not really. The service is there, but it is not being offered by CPA firms because it would be too expensive, and it also could not be done by the internal staffs themselves.

COULD YOU OFFER IT AT A COST SAVINGS OR MORE EFFICIENT THAN THE COMPANIES THEMSELVES, OR THE CPA FIRMS?

Yes.

THEN IT IS REALLY A QUESTION OF MARKETING THE SERVICES?

Yes.

BUT YOU COULD SOLVE THAT PROBLEM?

I believe so.

THEN WHY NOT DO IT?

I do not want to fail.

HOW DO YOU KNOW YOU WOULD FAIL?

I don't know that I would fail, but I might.

YOU MIGHT ALSO GET HIT BY A CAR BUT THAT DOES NOT STOP YOU FROM GOING OUTSIDE ON THE STREET DOES IT?

True.

AS MUCH AS I HATE SAYING IT, WUM IS RIGHT. SO, WHAT IF YOU FAIL? WHAT IF YOU SUCCEED? I PERSONALLY THINK THAT PEOPLE ARE MORE AFRAID OF SUCCEEDING THAN THEY ARE OF FAILING. THAT IS WHAT KEEPS PEOPLE FROM TRYING. SO, WHAT IF YOU FAIL? DO I NEED TO TELL YOU THE STORY OF ABRAHAM LINCOLN?

No, I know all about his failures, and his successes.

THE FAILURE IS IN NOT TRYING, NOT IN FAILING. IF YOU ARE SUCCESSFUL, YOU WILL BE ABLE TO SAY THAT YOU HAVE CREATED AND BUILT SOMETHING OF YOUR OWN, AND IT IS VALUABLE, AND YOU HAVE ACCOMPLISHED SOMETHING THAT YOU, NO, WE, HAVE ALWAYS WANTED TO DO...BE A SUCCESS ON OUR OWN.

I AGREE!

The chances of success...

SHUT UP, DR. MIKE.

SHUT UP, DR. MIKE.

SHUT UP, DR. MIKE. YOU MORON!

Well, I guess I could...

IF YOU ARE GOING TO DO IT, DO IT, BUT PUT ALL YOUR ENERGY AND FAITH INTO IT. DO NOT DO IT HALF- HEARTEDLY.

I AGREE.

We are behind you 100%.

I will do it!

Good.

GREAT.

YOU CAN DO IT!

I will call the Yankees when I get to the office!

WHERE DID I FAIL?

Cars

(Beep Beep)

Author's Note: Cars are a necessary evil in our society. Nearly everyone that I know has a car, and drives it on a regular basis. They are a necessity, but they are not cheap. The discussion that follows is merely a tongue-in-cheek discussion about buying a different car. I hope it is helpful, but also enjoyable.

Michael...

YES?

I need advice on something. I want to buy a new car.

WHY?

Because my jeep is old, and it is costing me too much money.

DR. MIKE, YOUR PRESENCE IS REQUESTED.

I know. I heard. A few questions, Mike.

Shoot.

How much do you owe on the Jeep?

About six grand.

Another year to pay it off, correct?

Yes.

How much is it worth?

Probably about ten grand.

So, if you went to buy a new car, you would get maybe 4 grand as a down payment, correct?

Probably.

YOU ARE THE MOST VAGUE PERSON IN THIS FAMILY!

QUIET, WUM.

44

And what kind of a car would you like to get?

I was thinking of the Lexus SC430.

How much?

Retails at about 60 grand.

That is very funny.

What is?

You.

Why?

You want to buy a car for $60,000 with a down payment of $4,000.

No, that is just the value that I would get from my car if I traded it in. I could have more to add...

How much more?

I could probably put in another...five...maybe ten thousand more...

You are funny.

Why?

Do you think you can get a $60,000 car with a $14,000 down payment? You can't be serious...

LISTEN, PENCILNECK...

Mikey, stay out of this. Listen, Pencilneck...

45

Sticks and stones may break my bones, but words will never get you a $60,000 car!

Why?

In order for you to buy a car with that large of money to finance your payments would be more than 2 grand a month. Can you afford $2 grand going out for a car on your salary?

Maybe...

Really? Do you have some hidden stashes of money that I am unaware of?

No.

Have you talked this over with our Patti?

No, I wanted to surprise her.

THAT WOULD CERTAINLY SURPRISE HER ALL RIGHT. YOU WOULD HAVE TO AWAKEN HER WITH SMELLING SALTS, OR YOUR SWEAT SOCKS.

I would agree with Wum. That would not be a good surprise...

TRUE. MIKE, I KNOW THEY ARE RIGHT.

Okay, then what kind of a car should I get?

Why get a new one?

Because the old one costs too much to upkeep...

How much have you spent on the car this year?

Five hundred on a radiator, two-eighty on the electrical, three hundred on a tune-up, and five oil changes at thirty-four ninety-five.

And how much did you spend in gas?

Twenty dollars a week...roughly a thousand dollars.

And how much is the payment?

Four fifty per month.

You spent roughly $1,300 on service, $1,000 in gas, and $5,400 in payments, and you want to spend $24,000 because the old car cost too much? That is absurd.

Yeah, well, maybe a $60,000 car does not make a whole lot of sense...

Wise decision.

How about a $50,000 car?

You are hopeless.

AT LEAST HE IS BEGINNING TO REALIZE WHAT HE CAN OR CANNOT AFFORD.

Yes, but he still needs to drop way down before he can afford that kind of a payment.

INDUBITABLY. MIKE, WHAT OTHER KINDS OF CARS WOULD YOU LIKE TO GET?

I was thinking of a 'Vette, or a Porsche...

It is my opinion that you are nuts.

Why?

Unless you are talking about a car that is 3-4 years old, you cannot get a Corvette or a Porsche for $50 thousand, let alone what it needs to be for your salary and payment structure.

IF WE ARE GOING TO TALK ABOUT GETTING A NEW CAR, I WANT TO PUT IN MY TWO CENTS.

THAT IS ABOUT ALL IT IS WORTH!

I WANT TO GET A BIG, VERY FAST, VERY POWERFUL MUSCLE CAR, PREFERABLY AN OLDER GTO, VINTAGE 1967, OR A RAM CHARGER, VINTAGE 1969, OR A ROAD RUNNER, VINTAGE 1972. I WOULD ALSO SETTLE FOR AN OLDS 442...

I am surrounded by idiots. If we are getting a new car, I suggest that we get one that is proven to the most reliable, most dependable car for the money that we have to spend.

THAT LEAVES OUT THE ROLLS. THANK HEAVENS! PERSONALLY, I THINK WE SHOULD GO FOR SOMETHING MORE FUN, LIKE A HUMMER.

FOR MY PART, I WOULD BE HAPPY WITH SOMETHING STYLISH AND SPORTY, BUT WITH THE ABILITY TO PERFORM. I WOULD PREFER THE CARRERA GT3.

Hello...people, we are not going to get a new car.

WHY NOT?

WHY NOT?

Why not?

WHY NOT?

I was only trying to get your ideas as to what we should do in a year or two, not immediately. You guys act as if you are going to go buy one tonight. Patti and I have not even considered the possibility of getting a new one.

DID YOU NOT ASK US FOR OUR ADVICE?

I asked you and you invited the others to this little soiree.

NOT ME. I INVITED MYSELF.

WHAT YOU DO NOT SEEM TO REALIZE IS THAT WHAT YOU SAY AND DO AFFECTS ALL OF US. THEREFORE, WE ALL MAY HAVE AN OPINION ON YOUR DECISION.

I get the feeling that I am stuck in a committee...

It is a proven fact that rule by committee does not work. Look at the former Soviet Union, for example.

That is why Lenin got rid of Trotsky and Stalin got rid of almost everyone. I may resort to those tactics if you guys do not quit arguing all of the time!

Language

(I know you are talking but I can't understand a word you are saying!)

Author's Note: Once when I was working as a CFO I was privy to a discussion between our operations manager, our customer service manager, our computer technician and myself. The operations manager and the customer service manager both spoke English as their natural language, and the computer technician was a Hispanic gentleman who spoke English as his second language, with, quite frankly, a bit of an accent as he had only been in this country for five years. The operations manager and the customer service manager were arguing about a particular idea, and the argument went on for twenty minutes. Neither of them seemed to understand what the other person was saying. Finally, our computer technician had enough, and in his accented English proceeded to explain, somewhat angrily, to each party separately what the other person was saying. When he finished, the operations manager and the customer service manager both looked at each other and said, somewhat sheepishly "Oh, now I understand, and that makes sense!" It was a very comical situation and has led me to suggest that even though we have a common language, that does not mean that we can communicate.

YOU ARE AN IDIOT! WHAT ARE YOU, A THIMBLE HEADED GHERKIN?

It is virtually impossible for you to know the intelligence quotient of that individual, Mikey. Furthermore, you called him things which he could never be. You called him a gherkin, which, as we all know is a small pickle. You also implied that he had a head, which is quite improbable. Finally, you mentioned that this nonexistent head was a thimble, which is quite unlikely.

I DO NO LIKE YOU! I WAS BEING POETIC.

Mikey, unless you are being funded by the National Endowment for the Arts, calling people names is not considered poetry.

THAT IS CORRECT. POETRY HAS BEEN CONSIDERED THROUGHOUT THE AGES AS ONE OF THE SIGNS OF A CULTURED AND CIVILIZED NATION. IT COULD EVEN BE SAID THAT EACH OF US ARE POETS IN THE SENSE THAT HOW WE LIVE OUR LIVES IS A MEASURE OF THE ERYTHEMATIC SENSE OF OUR DEEP-SEATED POETIC NATURES.

I AM SURROUNDED BY IDIOTS!

The term "thimble headed gherkin" was actually used in the comedic movie "*The Great Race*" starring Tony Curtis, Jack Lemmon, and Natalie Wood. It was when they were stranded on the iceberg and Max, played by the great Peter Falk, mentions to Professor Fate, played by Jack Lemmon, that it looks as if there is going to be storm after saying the phrase 'Red Sky at Morning, Sailor take warning," because they had awakened to a red sky. Professor Fate, in his best Mikey imitation, says, in retort, "You thimble headed gherkin! Do you know what the chances of a storm are in this area at this time" meaning that the chances obviously were low. But, as we all know, of course, a storm came in.

YOU ARE A VERITABLE FOUNTAIN OF KNOWLEDGE.

Why, thank you, Wum.

Dr. Mike does bring up an interesting point, however clothed in useless trivia it may be shrouded.

I object to the term 'useless.' I do not believe that knowledge, however trivial those of such pedantic nature may view it, is useful in some vein.

How is the knowledge of the movie "*The Great Race*" useful?

If you are playing *Trivial Pursuit*, or if you are on *Jeopardy*, or if you are trying to impress some woman in a bar, it could be useful.

USEFUL, AS IN TRYING TO CURE THIRD WORLD DEBT OR FEED STARVING PEOPLE IN ETHIOPIA...

Similar arguments, by the way, put forth by William Thacker's roommate in *Notting Hill* played by Rhy Ifans...

YOU QUOTE ONE MORE MOVIE AND I WILL MAKE SURE THAT YOU ARE NO LONGER PART OF ANY CONVERSATIONS THAT WE HAVE...

Calm down, Mikey. The fact of the matter is that Dr. Mike was commenting upon your use of the English language to express yourself. That is a very fascinating study and endeavor, as the ability to communicate is also the hallmark of civilization. But, I believe, the use of language to belittle or exalt oneself over one's neighbor is becoming more and more common, as is the use of violence as a means of settling disputes or discussions. It is also a sign as to the direction that our civilization is going.

WELL PUT, MIKE. THAT CERTAINLY IS AN ASTUTE OBSERVATION, ALTHOUGH PEOPLE HAVE BEEN SUGGESTING THIS FOR A LONG TIME. NOT TO BELITTLE OR DEMORALIZE YOU, BUT THAT IS NOT AN ORIGINAL THOUGHT OR IDEA.

Thank you.

SARCASM DOESN'T FIT YOU, MIKE.

I know. Language has always been an interesting study to me. I remember reading the description of Hitler by Winston Churchill. He never used a swear word, or obscene language, but you got the idea that Hitler was one of the most evil persons that God had ever created.

HITLER WAS ONE OF THE MOST EVIL PERSONS THAT GOD EVER CREATED.

The point is that language is a beautiful tool that can be a great source of pleasure, and can describe our world and everything in it without resorting to obscene or degrading. If you want to hear beautiful language, read Joseph Conrad...

Joseph Conrad is considered one of the greatest writers in the English Language, and he did not even learn English until he turned twenty-one.

Thank you. The point is that all language exists to communicate information from one human being to another.

Yes, but not only just to other humans. You communicate through language to other living creatures such as dogs, cats, etc. There is even some research to suggest that you can communicate with plants.

I ACTUALLY KNOW SOME PLANTS WHO UNDERSTAND MORE THAN SOME HUMAN BEINGS!

I THINK MOST OF US HAVE ACQUAINTANCES OF THAT NATURE, WUM. LANGUAGE CAN, AND SHOULD BE, USED TO FACILITATE INTERACTION BETWEEN ALL OF THE SPECIES ON THE PLANET.

Correct. It has never ceased to amaze me that human beings seem to think that they are the only species on the planet that has intelligence or language. Virtually every species communicates within its' own realm, and some use some very sophisticated methods to do so.

Yes, and I believe that they have their purpose for their language. I do not think, however, that we as a species use language to the best of our native ability.

What do you mean?

Well, how many four-letter words are used in everyday life?

LIKE LOVE, LIFE...

You know what I mean. The pervasiveness of obscenities in our society is increasing. You can hardly turn on the television without seeing the "f" word in movies. I think we have settled for the use of the obscene language so much that it has become part of the 'accepted' part of our culture.

what may be obscene to you may not be obscene to other people.

What?

WHAT?

What?

I simply said that what may be obscene to you may not be obscene to other people. Not everyone has the "high ideals" that you do, Mike

EVERYONE, I WOULD LIKE TO INTRODUCE YOU, UH, TO SOMEONE WE WILL CALL MR. MIKE. HE IS, SHALL I SAY, THE 'DOWNER' SIDE OF US.

55

i prefer to think of myself as the reality of us. after all, it is a jungle out there. and language simply reflects the rest of society. society is vicious, brutal, and obscene. therefore, language should reflect society.

You weren't kidding, were you Michael...

WHERE DID WE PICK THIS GUY UP? MIKE, DID YOU FORGET TO TAKE SOME PROZAC OR SOMETHING?

I do not need drugs...at least I haven't up till now.

MR. MIKE IS SIMPLY A MANIFESTATION OF WHAT WE ALL GO THROUGH. EVERYONE GETS DISCOURAGED NOW AND THEN. IT IS WHEN MR. MIKE DOMINATES AND CONTROLS MOST OF THE TIME THAT IT CAN BE A PROBLEM. RIGHT, MR. MIKE?

sure. whatever you say. but the fact is that language is rotten because society is basically rotten. everyone is out for himself, or herself. nobody cares about others, crime is rampant, people lie, cheat and steal every day. it is not a nice place...

Whoa, boy. Michael, how often does he come out?

NOT OFTEN. ONLY WHEN WE GET INTO THE "BLUE FUNK". BUT HE DOES HAVE A POINT. LANGUAGE DOES REFLECT SOCIETY, AND OUR SOCIETY HAS BECOME MORE LAX IN WHAT IT CONSIDERS PROPER. AS A RESULT, OBSCENITIES ARE NO LONGER CONSIDERED TABOO IN CONVERSATION ANY MORE WHEREAS IT WAS ONLY ACCEPTED BEFORE WHEN A PERSON WAS REALLY ANGRY OR LOST CONTROL. BUT THEN, AND ONLY THEN, AS LONG AS IT DID NOT HAPPEN OFTEN. BUT, NO MORE.

So, one possibly could make the argument that if we were to correct society, we could then correct language.

assuming society needs to be corrected...

I do not think there is much question about that, Mr. Mike.

It probably is much easier to correct language than society. There is even some research to suggest that by improving a person's language, conduct is also improved, such as in schools.

I think something needs to be done. Of course, I have always thought that society could not get worse, and then, it gets worse. However, now that I have seen Mr. Mike in action, I think that I will use whatever control I have to make sure he does not get out very often. That might even help to bring language and society back up to where I think it should be!

Good idea.

ALL RIGHT!!!!!!

$#& you.*

Education

(Does PhD really mean 'Piled Higher and Deeper?')

Author's Note: I believe in education, but I think there is things that could be improved in the process. Having taught for a while, I also think that it is a very noble profession. I have often had the following thoughts in my mind about education, and the resultant quandary in which we, as a society, find ourselves.

MIKE, DO YOU HAVE ANY DESIRES TO GO BACK TO SCHOOL?

What?

DO YOU HAVE ANY DESIRE TO GO BACK TO SCHOOL?

I already have a graduate degree, and I have enough credits for another degree if I ever wanted to get it. What do I need to go back to school for?

I WAS JUST WONDERING. I KNOW THAT WE HAVE OFTEN THOUGHT OF TEACHING, AND GETTING YOUR PHD WOULD ALLOW YOU TO TEACH AT A COLLEGIATE LEVEL.

I could teach high school now if I wanted to teach. I have passed the California C Best test for teachers, so I could teach now if I wanted. Plus, I could teach night school if I really wanted to.

YES, BUT TEACHING AT A COLLEGE HAS ALWAYS APPEALED TO YOU, HAS IT NOT?

Of course, it has. I think that that would be the ideal situation in life.

THEN WHY NOT DO IT?

BECAUSE HE DOES NOT WANT TO GET AWAY FROM THE BIG BUCKS HE EARNS IN BUSINESS FOR THE LOW PAYING SALARY OF A TEACHER.

IS THAT RIGHT?

You know the answer to that.

WHY IS IT THAT OUR SOCIETY CLAIMS TO VALUE EDUCATION YET OUR COLLEGE GRADUATES OFTEN EARN LESS THAN THOSE WHO ARE NOT COLLEGE GRADUATES?

Give me an example…

The average salary of a teacher in the United States is $59,000 a year. A plumber makes $80,000 per year with overtime, and teamsters make $65,000 a year.

Yes, but teachers work in a nicer environment…

SOME SCHOOLS I WOULD NOT CONSIDER AS A "NICE ENVIRONMENT". KNIVES, THREATS, AND OTHER HAZARDS ARE NOT NICE TO WORK WITH.

Understood, but that is not exactly a college environment, correct?

I SUPPOSE.

THEN, IT REALLY IS A MATTER OF MONEY?

Yes, to a certain extent, it is.

WHAT DO YOU MEAN "TO A CERTAIN EXTENT"?

Money is not the only factor. Time, age, opportunity, and other factors exist.

LIKE WHAT*?*

MIKEY, WHY ARE YOU SO ANGRY ABOUT MIKE NOT GOING TO SCHOOL?

BECAUSE HE HAS TALENT IN TEACHING, AND COULD HAVE BEEN A GREAT COLLEGE TEACHER, BUT HE TOOK THE EASY WAY OUT.

I did not. I chose to go to work after the MBA because I had a wife and child, and I thought that it would have been a good career. Looking back, Mikey is right. But that is a moot point. To go back now would be hard.

BUT NOT IMPOSSIBLE.

No, but suppose I did. I could get my PHD in finance after four years, then I would be sixty-five years old. But there are also is a limit on the number of teaching positions available at colleges. I am not sure, but I do not believe that there would be too many offers for a sixty five year-old college professor without tenure.

EXCUSES, EXCUSES, EXCUSES.

No, they are valid reasons. I am no longer a spring chicken, and I make good money, and time and opportunity are all, well, shall we say a piece of the puzzle.

BUT I WILL BET YOU DOLLARS TO DOUGHNUTS THAT IT IS THE MAIN EXCUSE.

I am sixty years old, with a large mortgage, and no retirement to speak of. If I were independently wealthy then the decision to go back to school is different. But I am not independently wealthy, nor does it look to be in my future. So, I will be content doing what I am doing. Just because I do not go to school does not mean that I will stop learning. I have a whole bunch of things to learn, and do.

YOU HAVE JUST MADE THE ARGUMENT FOR NOT GETTING AN EDUCATION...

Not necessarily. There are obviously certain jobs that are closed to you if you do not have a college education, or specialized training. A perfect example is a doctor. In order to be a doctor you have to go to college, then medical school, then spend years as an intern, resident, etc. That is all part of education, but that is what you have to do to be a doctor. To flip burgers at a fast food restaurant requires little schooling. It all depends upon what it is that you want to do.

WHAT IS IT THAT YOU WOULD LIKE TO DO?

I want to play centerfield for the New York Yankees

what an ^%$#%**!

I THINK THAT WE HAVE BEEN OVER THIS BEFORE.

War

("Why can't we all just get along?" – Rodney King)

Author's Note: War, as a noun, is defined as follows: "a state of armed conflict between different nations or states or different groups within a nation or state." According to my phone, this definition comes from Oxford. I assume, quite loosely, that this meant to say The Oxford Dictionary. At any rate, the concept that is suggested by the definition has been a part of human nature ever since…well, there were humans. For example, in the Bible we read that one of Adam and Eve's children, Cain, killed his brother Abel (Genesis 4:1-8). As a person that believes in the basic goodness of human beings, it grieves me to see the continuous wars and contentions that exist in our world. The pain and suffering of our brothers and sisters all over the world is painful and hard to imagine. Even though the following tries to approach the subject with humor, in reality there is no real humor in war. Maybe the humor is in the approach of the people who perpetuate the wars, and their thought processes.

i am really confused about the world situation right now.

WHY? IT SEEMS JUST LIKE BUSINESS AS USUAL, IF WAR IS A BUSINESS.

wum, i am not talking to you. i want an intelligent response. why do you suppose that there are so may wars in the world today?

Technically, they are not wars. They are regional conflicts!

SHUT UP!

People, can I have some order here please. There is no need to add to the world's problems by starting a war...

Regional conflict.

CALLATE, TONTO! SOMETIMES I LAPSE INTO MY NATIVE TONGUE.

SPANISH IS NOT YOUR NATIVE TONGUE, MORON!

shut up!

...regional conflict amongst ourselves.

ACTUALLY, THAT DOES BRING TO THE FRONT ONE OF THE PROBABLE CAUSES OF WAR.

Regional conflict.

IS IT POSSIBLE FOR US TO PUT DR. PINHEAD HERE IN A LOCKER OR SOMETHING? WAR...

Regional conflict.

...IS MY FAVORITE TOPIC. I AM GOING TO HURT YOU SOOOO BAD!

CHILDREN, BEHAVE. MIKEY, DO YOU NOT LIKE DR. MIKE?

I DON'T LIKE ANYONE.

JUST ON GENERAL GROUNDS, OR IS YOUR DISLIKE FOCUSED ON EVERYONE AND ALL THINGS?

IN OUR LITTLE UNIVERSE, POPULATION SIX, I DO NOT LIKE ANY OF YOU, NOR DO I LIKE ANYTHING ABOUT YOU.

HEY MR. WONDERFUL, THE FEELING IS MUTUAL.

Sure is.

you are a jerk.

KISS MY...

People, I will shut us down unless you guys start playing nice.

THANK YOU, MIKE. MIKEY, DO YOU DISLIKE SOME OF US LESS THAN OTHERS?

YES, BUT YOU ALL ARE JUST A COLLECTION OF ATTITUDES.

Then it is attitude that creates the dislike?

THAT AND A MILLION OTHER TINY LITTLE THINGS THAT DRIVE ME NUTS. I HAVE LIVED WITH YOU

GUYS FOR SIXTY YEARS, AND I AM GETTING TIRED OF IT.

CAN YOU GIVE US AN EXAMPLE?

SURE. MICHAEL, YOU THINK THAT YOU ARE BETTER THAN THE REST OF US. MIKE, YOU LET THINGS GET AWAY FROM YOU AND YOU DO NOT STAND UP FOR YOURSELF. WUM, YOU HAVE UNDENIABLY THE WORST SENSE OF HUMOR, BUT YOU THINK THAT YOU ARE FUNNY. DR. MIKE, YOU ARE A PURVEYOR OF USELESS STATISTICAL INFORMATION THAT NOBODY, I MEAN, NOBODY CARES ABOUT. AND MR. MIKE, ALL YOU WANT TO DO IS WORRY ABOUT EVERYTHING, AND WE AIN'T BIG ENOUGH TO HANDLE IT ALL. I TELL YA, YOU GUYS ARE A BASKET CASE, EVEN WITHOUT ME!

AHAH!

WHAT DO YOU MEAN "AHAH?"

is that "ahah" or "a hah"?

63.9% of people who say "ahah" say that because they think that they know the reasons why the person said what they did in order to get the response "ahah".

MIKEY, IF YOU WANT TO HIT DR. MIKE, I WILL HOLD HIM...

AHAH!

I think I may have to step in here before this gets too far gone. Let me sum up what my experience tells me. Mikey, if you were a country you would be at war...

Regional conflict.

...for a number of reasons. One may be because you felt that another country did not respect you. Another may be because they may have something you do not. A reason may be because of some slight in the past that has crystallized into a hatred of one of the other countries. A reason may be because you feel it is your right to be the dominant personality in the universe, and you know best. It may even be because the other country does not have the right to exist, and they are an evil parasite encroaching on your inherent value system, and must be destroyed at all cost. Another reason could be that you just like war...

Regional conflict.

...regional conflict to such an extent that you want it to be your modus operandi. And finally, you may use regional conflict...

War. OOOPS! MY BAD!

...just because you do not like living next to the same persons, us, for sixty years, and you want it to change.

MIKEY, PEOPLE HAVE BEEN ASKING THOSE QUESTIONS EVER SINCE THE TERM OR CONDITION BECAME THE PLAGUE FOR HUMANS. IF WE COULD ANSWER THE QUESTIONS TRUTHFULLY, THEN MAYBE WE COULD FINALLY END UP WITH A WAY TO OUTLAW THAT TERM.

THEN WAR...

Regional Conflict.

...IS A BAD THING.

WAR IS NOT GOOD FOR CHILDREN AND OTHER LIVING THINGS. BUT SOMETIMES IT IS NECESSARY. NO ONE WOULD QUESTION

THE FACT THAT STOPPING HITLER IN WORLD WAR II WAS A GOOD THING. HE WAS OUT FOR WORLD DOMINATION WITH A PHILOSOPHY BASED UPON RACE AND A BASIC LACK OF FREEDOM OF CHOICE.

Wars...

Regional conflicts.

...have been fought for every cause imaginable. Property, economics, rights, freedoms, slavery, and my personal favorite, religion. I have no doubt that virtually every difference in human nature has been the reason for a war...

Regional conflict.

...throughout human history. What it boils down to, however, in my simplistic view of the world, is that those things happen because of difference, prejudice, lack of tolerance, and the inability of human beings to recognize the God given gift of free agency. Every human has the right to choose how they want to be.

SO, IF I CHOOSE TO SWING MY FIST AT YOU, THAT IS MY CHOICE?

AND IF YOU HIT HIM, HE HAS THE RIGHT TO SWING BACK. YOUR RIGHT TO SWING YOUR FIST ENDS WHERE HIS NOSE BEGINS.

And I will probably choose to swing back at you, and so forth. And if there were others in my universe that thought you were not a nice person, they would help me, if they chose.

Then we would be at war!

REGIONAL CONFLICT.

REGIONAL CONFLICT.

regional conflict.

Regional conflict.

REGIONAL CONFLICT.

The Universe

("Our object collision budget is $3 million and,
pardon me sir, but it is a big ass sky." – Billy Bob
Thornton as the NASA chief in *Armageddon*)

Author's Note: Have you ever experienced a clear night where it just seemed that the night sky was very crowded with stars? What a wonderous thing to behold, and every time that I have this experience, I think of a lot of these thoughts that you will find in this portion of the book. I do wonder how big the Universe is, if there are any planets/solar systems like ours, if there are other beings out there, what they do for fun, and other such questions. Will we ever find the answers to these and a myriad of other questions that we humans have been asking for eons of time? I do not know, but it is fun to discuss.

Dr. Mike, how big is the universe?

No one knows, and since no one knows, it is particularly difficult for me to have that information, or even give a guesstimate as to it's size.

Mr. Spock would know…

Mr. Spock was a fictional character on a tv series in the 60's and in a number of forgettable movies since. I doubt that Leonard Nimoy or Zachary Quinto, who both played Mr. Spock, would even hazard a guess.

NOT ALL OF THE STAR TREK MOVIES WERE FORGETTABLE…

Name one.

STAR TREK II: THE WRATH OF KHAN WAS PRETTY GOOD, ALTHOUGH I WAS ROOTING FOR KHAN TO WIN AND GIVE THOSE SMUG CRETINS THEIR COME-UPPANCE.

PERSONALLY, MY FAVORITE WAS *STAR TREK IV: THE VOYAGE HOME.* COURSE IT WAS ONLY BECAUSE OF CATHERINE HICKS THAT IT WAS ANY GOOD. I DO LOVE LEFT-HANDED BLONDES.

YEAH, BUT SHE IS DIFFERENT. I SAW HER ON LETTERMAN ONCE AND SHE ANSWERED QUESTIONS AS IF SHE WERE DR. MIKE.

It doesn't matter. She is a beautiful woman and her smile is dazzling. I agree with Wum.

THANK YOU' MIKE. GREAT MINDS THINK ALIKE.

"GREAT MINDS????????"

Let's get back to the question...how big is the universe?

In our very limited database of knowledge, there is no such number that is an actual number that says "The universe is XXXX."

ONE OF THE REASONS GIVEN IS THAT THERE IS NO WAY WE AS HUMANS CAN KNOW OR EVEN INTELLIGENTLY MEASURE SUCH AN EXPANSE SIMPLY BECAUSE WE LACK THE TOOLS TO DEFINE THESE THINGS IN AN UNDERSTANDABLY PRECISE MEASUREMENT, AND THAT IS WHAT HUMANS LOOK FOR: THE QUANTIFICATION OF THINGS. WE QUANTIFY BECAUSE WE HAVE A HARD TIME DEALING WITH THE ABSTRACTS, SUCH AS THE ENDS OF THE UNIVERSE, OR TIME OR SUCH THINGS.

What about Einstein?

WHAT ABOUT EINSTEIN?

Didn't he understand the universe?

Professor Einstein didn't so much understand it as to give us ways to look at things, and help us understand our world in relation to the rest of God's creations...

i thought einstein was an atheist.

MANY PEOPLE BELIEVED HE WAS DUE TO HIS THEORIES. AS A MAN, EINSTEIN DEEPLY BELIEVED IN GOD, AND APPRECIATED HIS HANDIWORK. BUT A DISCUSSION ABOUT GOD IS ANOTHER SUBJECT. UNLESS WE DEVELOP THE ABILITY TO GRASP CONCEPTS GREATER THAN WE HAVE NOW, WE MAY NEVER TRULY BE ABLE TO UNDERSTAND THE UNIVERSE, HOW BIG IT IS, HOW IT BEGAN, AND HOW IT WILL END, IF IT EVER DOES.

WE KNOW HOW IT BEGAN...WITH A BIG BANG!

WHO CAUSED THE BIG BANG?

WHAT?

WHO, OR WHAT, CAUSED THE BIG BANG?

I DON'T KNOW.

WERE YOU THERE WHEN IT HAPPENED?

IT HAPPENED MILLIONS OF YEARS AGO! HOW COULD I HAVE BEEN AROUND?

DO YOU KNOW ANYONE THAT WAS AROUND WHEN IT HAPPENED?

no one was around when it happened...

THEREIN LIES THE WHOLE CRUX OF THE MATTER, DOESN'T IT? THE BIG BANG THEORY IS JUST THAT – A THEORY.

so is creationism.

I think there may be a little disagreement on that. Creationism implies an intelligent first cause, whether you call it 'god', or 'higher power', or 'whatever'. I think that there is probably more logic to suggest this line of thinking than to suggest that it all came about as an explosion...

CORRECTAMUNDO. PERFECT EXAMPLE ARE THE KIDS WHEN THEY WERE TEENAGERS. GETTING THEM TO DO ANYTHING WAS LIKE GETTING TWO PIECES OF WOOD TO HAMMER THEMSELVES INTO A BUILDING. IT JUST AIN'T GONNA HAPPEN!

FINALLY! WE AGREE!

KNOCK IT OFF, YOU TWO. THERE IS NOTHING WRONG WITH THE KIDS. ALL TEENAGERS ARE LIKE THAT.

THAT'S RIGHT! IT IS LIKE THE OLD JOKE ABOUT ABRAHAM AND ISAAC IN THE BIBLE. A GUY ASKS HOW DO YOU KNOW THAT ISAAC WASN'T A TEENAGER? CAUSE IF HE WAS, IT WOULDN'T HAVE BEEN A SACRIFICE!

DARN STRAIGHT!

Come on guys, kids weren't that bad. Maybe it was just that we are bad parents...

no, they are that bad...

Back to the universe...

Was that a movie...

THAT WAS *BACK TO THE FUTURE*, YOU IDIOT.

Actually, there were three movies of that name. Which brings up an interesting dilemma...

AS ON THE 'HORNS OF A'?

If a dilemma is not an animal, how can it have horns?

YOU HAVE NO SENSE OF HUMOR...

how do we know there is not an animal that is called a dilemma?

According to the dictionary, there is no animal named 'dilemma'.

is the dictionary the sum total of knowledge of the human race?

OF COURSE NOT...

then you do admit the possibility that there may be an animal, somewhere, called a dilemma?

No. The language that we speak does not identify an animal that is called a 'dilemma", or is referred to in any other known language that which would be translated as 'dilemma'.

does our language include all of human knowledge?

No.

does our language know of all of the animal species that exist, that may exist, or that have ever existed anywhere in the universe?

Of course not. No human has that knowledge...

'dilemma', of course, is in the dictionary?

Yes.

so, there is a possibility that, theoretically, there could be an animal somewhere actually named a 'dilemma'?

I guess there is that possibility, although from a linguist's point of view, 'dilemma' may not be a good name for an animal because of what it is defined by, in the lexicon of the society using that language.

is 'big bang' in the dictionary?

Yes.

i rest my case.

ME TOO.

Taxes

(The reason for high taxes is to keep folks from spending their money foolishly on things they want so the government can spend it foolishly on things other folks want."

-Author Unknown)

Author's Note: I am certain that all of my readers have experienced the following if they took the opportunity to do their own taxes. I imagine that it is a common experience all over the United States between April 1 and April 15. For those of you who have shared this frustration, enjoy. For those of you who have never experienced this moment, enjoy what you have missed!

&^%$^&@#$!!!!!

Mikey, what is going on?

**I AM IN THE PROCESS OF DOING MY TAX RETURN.
*%^$#%^%$!!!!**

Come on, it cannot be that bad, is it?

**WELL, ACTUALLY IT IS. I BARELY HAVE ENOUGH
TO LIVE ON SINCE THE GOVERNMENT IS KIND
ENOUGH TO TAKE MOST OF MY EXCESS CASH.**

IT COULD BE WORSE...THEY COULD TAKE ALL OF IT!

SHUT UP, FUNNYMAN!

Mikey, settle down. We go through this every year. You have to understand that
it is not reasonable to go nuts every year when you do the taxes. You have to get
in the mind-set of "it's that time of year and I am not going to let it bother me".
After all, it is inevitable like death and...

TAXES.

REAL FUNNY.

WHAT SEEMS TO BE THE PROBLEM?

IT'S TAX TIME AGAIN AND MIKEY ISN'T A HAPPY
TAXPAYER.

*QUITE FRANKLY, I AM SURPRISED THAT NOT MORE PEOPLE
GO THROUGH THIS AT THIS TIME OF THE YEAR.*

Conversations with Myself

I actually met a guy who worked for the IRS once. He interviewed for a position with the company that I was with, and all he did in the interview was argue with my boss about taxes. Needless to say, he didn't get the position.

DUH!!!

I CANNOT IMAGINE ANYONE ACTUALLY ADMITTING TO ANYONE THAT THEY WORK FOR THE IRS...

I CAN. ACCORDING TO PRESIDENT GEORGE HERBERT WALKER BUSH, THE IRS IS PART OF A GENTLER, KINDER FEDERAL GOVERNMENT.

*&^%$%^&#@!!!!

Now Mikey, get a hold of yourself. Good. Now explain to me why you are upset?

&&&^%$!!!!

I think we need to have this conversation without Mikey. Why don't you go find some more deductions?

*&$%#@!!!! OKAY.

TAXES ARE NECESSARY SO THAT THOSE INDIVIDUALS WHO SERVE US IN GOVERNMENT CAN PROVIDE FOR THE COMMON ITEMS THAT WE ALL RELY UPON IN OUR SOCIETY. THINGS SUCH AS THE MILITARY TO PROTECT US, THE HIGHWAYS AND BY-WAYS OF AMERICA. ALL OF THOSE FUN THINGS THAT WE CANNOT DO FOR OURSELVES...

LIKE WELFARE?

There are certain aspects of government that must help people who do not have the means or abilities to take care of themselves. They sometimes take the form of social programs, and the debate over the usefulness, or lack thereof, is a constant debate in a free society.

I UNDERSTAND ALL OF THIS. YOU SEEM TO FORGET THAT I HAVE A DEGREE IN POLITICAL SCIENCE, WITH A MASTERS DEGREE IN BUSINESS ADMINISTRATION.

THEN, OF COURSE YOU UNDERSTAND THE NEED FOR TAXES. THERE ARE CERTAIN THINGS THAT WE HAVE TO 'PAY FOR' THAT THE GOVERNMENT PROVIDES FOR US, AND LIKE MOST EVERYTHING IN THIS WORLD, MOST OF THEM TAKE MONEY.

That is fine, but I think Mikey's frustration, and a lot of other peoples', is that a lot of money comes out in the form of taxes, and I am not sure that those in the government practice fiscal conservatism.

I THINK WE HAVE MORE TAXES THAN 'CARTER HAS PILLS" TO USE AN OLD PHRASE. WE HAVE FEDERAL TAXES, STATE TAXES, LOCAL TAXES, PROPERTY TAXES, SALES & USE TAXES, EXCISE TAXES, INHERITANCE TAXES, ESTATE TAXES, AND THE HITS JUST KEEP ON COMING!

That is because we have multiple forms of governments in our complex society.

WHY?

You know the answer to that.

OH YEAH! I FORGOT. IT IS SO WE DON'T KNOW WHO IS PICKING OUR POCKET AT ANY PARTICULAR TIME...

Funny.

Let's look at it from a logical point of view. As members of American society, we receive benefits from simply living in this great country. Using the transportation system as an example, the highways are wonderful (except for a few billion potholes here and there) and we can travel anywhere that we want to. In order to do that, we need a central government that can coordinate the building of highways that lock the various parts of the country together for commerce and for the simple pleasure of going on vacation. If there were no central agency doing this, the roads in let's say, Arkansas, would look vastly different than the roads in New York…

THE ROADS IN ARKANSAS DO LOOK DIFFERENT THAN THE ROADS IN NEW YORK.

You know what I mean. Have you ever run across a road where a sign says "Ending County Maintenance of this road"? Suddenly you are on a dirt or gravel road because the person responsible for the road at that time has yet to pave it. Without a central system, the whole highway system would be a patchwork of various roads and surfaces. It would not be the most efficient way of doing things…

ASSUMING, OF COURSE, THAT THE GOVERNEMNT IS EFFICIENT.

ONCE AGAIN, I UNDERSTAND THAT. BUT WHY DO THEY HAVE TO TAKE SO MUCH OF MY MONEY? I FEEL THAT I AM PAYING FOR ALL OF THE ROADS IN CALIFORNIA!

We have a graduated tax system, wherein the more money that you make the more taxes you will pay as a percentage.

Approximately 20% of the individuals pay 80% of the individual taxes.

The reason for a graduated system is the thought that the more benefit you receive the more you are using the services and therefore the more you should pay.

I GIVE 10% TO MY CHURCH, AND I PAY MORE THAN THAT IN TAXES. WHY SHOULD I PAY MORE TO THE GOVERNMENT THAN I DO TO GOD?

I THINK THAT MANY PEOPLE USE THIS ARGUMENT TO LIMIT TAXES TO A FLAT AMOUNT FOR EVERYONE. BUT I THINK THE REAL QUESTION THAT MAY BE ASKED IS THIS: 'DOES GOD REALLY MIND BEING PAID LESS THAN THE GOVERNMENT?'. I THINK THAT HE WOULD LIKE TO BE KEPT OUT OF THAT ARGUMENT. 'RENDER UNTO CAESAR THAT WHICH IS CAESAR'S, AND UNTO GOD THAT WHICH IS GOD'S' (MATTHEW 22:21).

SINCE GOD CREATED EVERYTHING, WE THEN SHOULD NOT GIVE ANYTHING TO CAESAR. BESIDES, I AM NOT A ROMAN.

Strangely enough, some have made that argument also, saying that the FEDS or any other government agency do not have the right in our constitution to levy an income tax, which is the source of Mikey's frustration.

LOOK, I DO NOT HAVE A PROBLEM PAYING MY 'FAIR SHARE' BUT I DO HAVE ISSUES IN PAYING MORE THAN THAT. ESPECIALLY WHEN I SEE MY TAX DOLLARS GO FOR SUBSIDIZING PEOPLE WHO COULD WORK, BUT THEY DON'T NEED TO BECAUSE THEY GET A WELFARE CHECK OR FOUR. OR HOW ABOUT THE CITY EMPLOYEE WHO GETS A 9% RAISE TWO YEARS IN A ROW WHEN I HAVE HAD TO REDUCE MY SALARY TO KEEP MY BUSINESS GOING SO THAT MY EMPLOYEES DO NOT LOSE THEIR JOBS. IT IS NOT FAIR.

IF LIFE WERE FAIR, I WOULD HAVE BEEN BORN RICH INSTEAD OF SO DARN GOOD-LOOKIN'!

Dream on, Wum.

WHAT ABOUT THOSE WONDERFUL SOCIAL PROGRAMS THAT PERHAPS I DO NOT BELIEVE IN, BUT MY 'GOVERNMENT' DOES THEM ANYWAY BECAUSE SOME MISGUIDED ELECTED CHIMPANZEE FEELS THAT IS THE WAY HE/SHE WANTS IT TO BE?

NOW YOU HAVE HIT THE EXACT PROBLEM OF A DEMOCRATIC SOCIETY. YOU HAVE THE RIGHT TO VOTE, OR NOT VOTE, FOR SAID MISGUIDED CHIMPANZEE IN THE NEXT ELECTION. IF ENOUGH PEOPLE BELIEVE THE WAY THAT YOU DO, SAID MISGUIDED CHIMPANZEE WOULD THEN NOT BE ELECTED. SO, YOU HAVE THE RIGHT TO VOTE, OR NOT VOTE, AND TO TELL YOUR ELECTED OFFICIALS JUST EXACTLY WHAT YOU THINK OF THEM. IF ENOUGH OF YOU GET TOGETHER AND TELL THE CHIMPANZEE WHAT YOU WANT, THEY WILL DO WHATEVER YOU WANT.

he is correct. most political figures are more concerned about re-election than anything else. if enough people tell him that they are not going to vote for him because he did 'xyz', then the chimp will not do 'xyz' again.

Mr. Mike is right. The best way to make your voice heard is to get involved in the political process. So, Mikey, what you need to do is to write your congressperson and explain to them that you want them to be a little more responsible with your taxes.

YEAH, LIKE THAT IS GOING TO HELP! HAVE YOU HEARD BACK FROM A CONGRESSPERSON?

Actually, yes, I have. He wrote back and told me that he was going to have to raise my taxes to pay for people to answer all of the letters that were sent to him.

Professional Sports

(Games or Business, or Both?)

Author's Note: I love sports. I have played virtually every sport known to mankind in my many years on the earth. I would play all day on Saturday, then I would get up Sunday morning before everyone else, grab a bowl of cereal, and lay down and read the sports section, start to finish. Every word. As a result, I would play the appropriate sport during the appropriate season. My favorite sport was basketball (growing up in Indiana, what else is new!), but I believe I had the best chance to succeed in the sport of baseball. Did I dream of playing professionally? Yes! Did I try? Yes, but I was a lousy hitter. I could not hit a curve ball. My fielding was superb, but my hitting was definitely not to the standard of even mediocre high school players. But I have continued my interest in sports with my children and grandchildren. I go to as many of their games as I can, and I can unequivocally suggest that among the parents, most of the fathers truly believe that their child will make it to the professional ranks, in whatever sport they are trying. Granted the older the player, the less the number of parents feel that way, and they try to encourage other sports. But I digress. I watch professional sports, but not as much as I did as a youngster. As you will see by the following, I believe I have issues with professional sports. But honestly, if my grandson goes pro, that will abruptly change!

MIKE, WHY ARE PROFESSIONAL SPORTS SO IMPORTANT TO AMERICANS?

In the movie "Patton" which, by the way, won the Academy Award for Best Picture in 1970, George C. Scott as Patton says that "Americans have never lost a war" and that "Americans love winners". Perhaps it is the thrill of competition that is inherent among America that we love to compete, we love to win, and we love to be winners.

George C. Scott also won the Academy Award for Best Actor for that role. In fact, "Patton" won five Academy Awards and was nominated for five others. What a great movie.

Yes, it was. Many memorable scenes, and George C. Scott was fantastic, even though he did not accept the award.

WHAT????

He refused to accept the award because he did not believe that awards were fair to all of the hard working and talented people that did not get recognized. He called it a 'goddam meat parade'.

I AM PRETTY SURE THAT HIS STATUETTE WAS IN HIS POSSESSION WHEN HE DIED...

Well, you would be wrong. It is now in the George C. Marshall Foundation at the Virginia Military Institute in Lexington, Virginia. That is where General George S. Patton went to school. It was donated several weeks after the awards ceremony.

what does this have to do with professional sports?

Not a thing. Mr. Mike, do you like professional sports?

HE LIKES THE FACT THAT THERE ARE LOSERS!

Be quiet Wum. If you are a part of me, then you probably like professional sports, correct?

not really. i do not like the fact that they are so all encompassing in our society. i went to a dodger game a while ago and saw some fans attack a guy wearing a giants jersey. they have become way too important and divisive to our country.

IS IT BECAUSE YOU SEE PROFESSIONAL SPORTS AS A BUSINESS?

Of course! It is a business. And it employs millions of people, not just the athletes.

if it were a business that just employed millions of people, i would be okay with it. but it has gone beyond that. now it is covered as news, not entertainment, and why some of these shows that are being televised are not 'sports', they are shows about a ridiculously small part of the sport. for example, the shows about predictions on the nfl draft — what a waste of time! or all of the shows with sports 'talking heads', more wasting of time. if i watch a game on tv, i do not need a 'former player' telling me what i saw, and what happened. those shows are getting to be as bad as the political shows, and i never thought anything involved with sports could stoop that low!

But people like those shows. If they didn't like them, they would not be on, correct?

i like sports, but whether or not the yankees win the world series is not going to define my life. this is, of course, my humble opinion.

WE ALL LIKE WATCHING SPORTS, DON'T WE?

yes.

YUP.

Yes, I do.

SI.

As long as it does not take away from other critical things in our life, such as Patti.

AMEN, BROTHER.

OH YEAH!

Absolutely!

i would have to agree with that.

WHAT WOULD YOU CHANGE ABOUT PROFESSIONAL SPORTS, IF YOU COULD?

All of the trash talking. It is everywhere, and at all levels. I watched one of my grandkids play, and I was appalled at the talk they allowed between players, and this was a basketball game between 9 year-old kids! These kids learn from the tv and the middle schoolers, the middle schoolers learn from the tv and the high school kids, the high school kids learn it from tv, travel ball, and the college players and the college players learn it from tv and the pros. I do not like it, and it will only get worse.

my issues have to do with the lack of sportsmanship, and it seems like it permeates all levels. maybe we should all go back to the playground, with no adults or referees!

I THINK ALL THE MONEY FOR SPORTS SHOULD BE TAKEN FOR MORE IMPORTANT THINGS, LIKE EDUCATION. IT IS A TRAVESTY THAT WE PAY OUR TEACHERS SO LITTLE, YET WE ALLOW PROFESSIONAL ATHLETES MILLIONS OF DOLLARS OVER THEIR CAREERS. IT REALLY MAKES ME ANGRY!!!!!!!!!

CALMATE, MIKEY.

However, Mikey, you have to admit that if a teacher had the skills in a sport that a professional athlete did, he, or she, would have probably gone in that direction. I mean, let's face it...we wanted to be a professional basketball player, but no one wants a slow footed, slightly athletic, five-foot nine-inch player with marginal skills. So, I found something else to do, that I liked and enjoyed.

YEAH, AND JUST THINK OF ALL OF THE MILLIONS WE MISSED OUT ON BECAUSE YOU WEREN'T GOOD ENOUGH!

dang dude. you blew it!

THANKS A LOT, MORON!

The statistical probability of a slow, marginally athletic, marginally skilled basketball player no more than five foot nine inches tall making it in the NBA is...well...next to impossible. You should have worked harder.

Come on guys! Give me a break.

WHAT OTHER THINGS WOULD YOU CHANGE ABOUT PROFESSIONAL SPORTS?

I WOULD BAN ALL PEOPLE WHO FIGHT FROM ALL STADIUMS. FOR EXAMPLE, THE SOCCER

HOOLIGANS IN ENGLAND. THEY SHOULD BAN THOSE IMBECILES FROM BEING ABLE TO ATTEND A GAME IN A PUBLIC STADIUM.

I would like to see the prices lowered so I could take my grandsons to a baseball game. I would also like to see more emphasis on sportsmanship, and not so much on winning.

DREAM ON!

yeah, like that is going to happen!

Sportsmanship, what is that?

THAT IS WHAT TEAMS HAVE THAT DO NOT HAVE TROPHIES FOR CHAMPIONSHIPS!

THAT IS NOT THE DEFINING CHARACTERISTIC OF SPORTSMANSHIP!

GROW UP!

what time does the game start?

YOU GOING TO WATCH IT?

Yes, we are.

WHY WASTE YOUR TIME?

my team is in last place. no way to go but up!

PROFESSIONAL SPORTS DOES REQUIRE REAL LOYALTY DOESN'T IT?

Only if your team is winning.

BUT IT IS FUN TO WATCH THE PEOPLE ON TV MAKE FOOLS OF THEMSELVES.

PART OF THE ATTRACTION?

YOU GOT IT BROTHER!

Swearing

("Profanity is the attempt of a feeble mind to express itself." - Winston Churchill)

Author's Note: As I have noted in the Introduction, my father, Dale J. Peterson, was the best man I have ever known. One of the qualities that I loved about him is that I never heard him use a swear word. Ever. I asked him once about that and he replied that "no man that I ever admired used them." I have tried to adopt that same mantra, although my self-control is not quite as great as his. But I am trying, just like my friend Mikey.

#$#&%!...

MIKEY?

WHAT?!!!!!

WHY ARE YOU SWEARING?

I HATE PAYING BILLS.

WHY?

BECAUSE THERE IS NEVER ENOUGH MONEY TO COVER THE BILLS.

SO? WHY SWEAR? IS THE USE OF FOUL LANGUAGE GOING TO CHANGE THE AMOUNT OF MONEY, OR THE AMOUNT OF BILLS THAT YOU HAVE?

NO.

THEN, I WILL ASK YOU AGAIN. WHY DO YOU SWEAR?

We only do it when we get angry.

BUT IF I AM THE ONE THAT GETS ANGRY, THEN I AM PROBABLY THE ONLY ONE THAT USES BAD LANGUAGE.

True.

I THINK THAT IS PROBABLY A CORRECT ASSESSMENT, MIKEY.

I think it is more of a reflex action than a character trait.

DON'T YOU MEAN CHARACTER 'FLAW' RATHER THAN CHARACTER 'TRAIT'?

Funny.

WUM MAY BE FACETIOUS, BUT IN THIS CASE HE MAY BE CORRECT.

The odds of a comedian making accurate statements is approximately...

SHUT UP!

BOYS, SETTLE DOWN. BUT I AM TALKING TO US ALL. WHY DO WE SWEAR?

It's a habit. A reflex action.

i like it. it shows we're human.

SO, IN YOUR ESTIMATION, MR. MIKE, SWEARING IS OKAY?

sure. everyone does it. have you watched television lately? you can hardly watch anything without hearing some sort of profanity.

JUST BECAUSE PEOPLE DO IT DOES NOT MAKE IT OKAY! JUST LOOK AT GOLF!

NOT EXACTLY A PERFECT EXAMPLE OF WHAT I THINK YOU WERE TRYING TO SAY, WUM. BUT I PERSONALLY DO NOT BELIEVE THAT THE USE OF PROFANITY EXHIBITS THE BEST USE OF HUMAN COMMUNICATION SKILLS.

I agree. When I hear people using profanity, especially in a public setting, it makes me feel uneasy.

TRUTH BE KNOWN, I THINK THAT I GET A LOT OF THIS FROM OUR DAD. I NEVER HEARD HIM UTTER A SWEAR WORD THAT I CAN REMEMBER. NEVER. COME TO THINK OF IT, MOST OF THE PEOPLE THAT I ADMIRE THE MOST ARE PEOPLE WHO NEVER SWEAR OR USE QUESTIONABLE LANGUAGE.

I just think there are better ways of expressing our emotions when things are not going our way...

SO, WHAT I AM HEARING IS THAT PRETTY MUCH EVERYONE WANTS ME TO STOP SWEARING, CORRECT?

Yes. That would be good.

YES, BUT I AM WORRIED YOU WILL NEVER SPEAK AGAIN...

TWIT!

you realize you just called all of us a name?

OOPS.

That would be nice from a statistical point of view. I wouldn't have to keep track of nearly so many words.

MIKEY, I BELIEVE THAT YOU CAN DO IT. DO YOU?

I GUESS.

NOT EXACTLY A ROUSING PROMISE TO CHANGE!

amen to that brother!

SO, IF I PROMISE TO NEVER AGAIN USE PROFANITY, EVEN ON A GOLF COURSE, YOU GUYS WILL NEVER SWEAR AGAIN, CORRECT?

NOPE.

As you are the agent of our anger, we can break the habit or flaw, and never use those words again, correct?

YUP.

Okay by me.

me too.

I think that would be great!

ME THREE.

SO, WE ARE ALL AGREED? FABULOUS. I LOVE IT WHEN A PLAN COMES TOGETHER!

THERE WAS A PLAN???????????????

There was a plan!

("Money makes the world go 'round..." Liza Minelli in *Cabaret*)

Author's Note: How many times have we thought about 'money'? We all have experienced thoughts about money, no matter how much, or how little, we have. I hope that the following will ease the reader's mind about money, and help all of us realize that money does not buy happiness. But it does help pay the bills!

I HATE PAYING BILLS!

ARE YOU SWEARING?

NO!

Good. Why do you hate paying bills?

BECAUSE THERE NEVER SEEMS TO BE ENOUGH MONEY!

Correct me if I am wrong, but isn't that a function of spending more than you take in?

LISTEN, EINSTEIN...

I am not Albert Einstein, in case you didn't know that!

SCORE ONE FOR THE DOC!

YOU KNOW WHAT I MEANT!

Yes, I did. But your tendency to get angry at seemingly irrelevant comments suggests that you are not entirely happy.

One of these days we are going to have to have a discussion on anger...

I AM NOT ANGRY ALL OF THE TIME!

NO, JUST MOST OF THE TIME...'ANYWHO', LET'S GET BACK TO THE SUBJECT AT HAND...MONEY!

YES, THE ROOT OF ALL EVIL!

Actually, the quote, most of the time misquoted by the way, is 'for the love of money is the root of all evil'. (1 Timothy 6:10)

SEMANTICS!!!!

Not really. The addition of the 'for the love of…' completely changes the meaning of both phrases.

CLARIFICATION, PLEASE.

If you suggest that 'money is the root of all evil', then the fact that it exists, or that you need it to survive is inherently a bad or evil thing because it (money) is, by itself, an evil. If, however, a person values the pursuit of money, or money itself, at the expense of other more important things such as love, humanity, family, kindness, etc. then THAT is evil and will not lead to one leading the life that God intended for you to live. That would mean that the pursuit of money above all other things is bad and/or evil.

And I think that makes a whole lot of sense. The thing that we are most focused upon is usually the thing that we love the most. If we are so focused on money, then we lose sight of what is most important in our life such as being a good person, a good father, a good neighbor, basically just a good human being.

i see your point, but i should point out that money is simply a means to an end, and it is necessary in this world to survive, yes?

Yes, it is necessary as we all need to survive and live, and, quite frankly, that takes money. But the question then becomes "How much do we need to survive"? For example, if Joe has enough to feed his family, pays the mortgage on the home, take care of the bills, go on a vacation every year, and even put some away for a rainy day, and he is happy about that, is that enough for him?

obviously, the answer is yes, that is fine for joe. but what if joe suddenly decides that he wants a second home in the bahamas, and a third home in aspen? are you saying that that is bad or evil? just

105

because a person wants a better life should not be considered a bad or evil thing.

THE ONLY THING BAD OR EVIL ABOUT THAT SCENARIO IS HIS CHOICE OF WHERE TO LIVE!

you, my friend, are an idiot!

THAT MAY BE THE CASE, BUT THE ISSUE MAY GO DEEPER THAN CHOICE OF LOCATION. IF JOE IS PERFECTLY CONTENT TO LIVE HIS LIFE WITHIN HIS MEANS AS STATED ABOVE BY DR. MIKE, WHY SHOULD WE SAY THAT THAT IS WRONG? BY THE SAME TOKEN, MR. MIKE IS ALSO CORRECT IS HIS ASSESSMENT THAT JUST WANTING A SECOND OR THIRD HOME IS NOT A BAD OR EVIL IDEA. HE MAY BE CORRECT IN HIS ASSUMPTION ABOUT WUM, HOWEVER...

right on!

WHAT?

JUST MESSING WITH YOU, WUM. SO, DR. MIKE, BOTH OF THESE SCENARIOS COULD SUGGEST THAT THEY COULD BE NOT CONSIDERED BAD OR EVIL, CORRECT?

I think you have to look at the motives behind the action before you could answer that. Let's suppose that Joe 1 is happy. He gets a visit from his sister and brother-in-law who happens to be very wealthy. Joe 1 looks at his sibling and says to himself 'Geez, am I a failure or what?' So, he starts working a second job, spends less time with his family, becomes too busy to help with the PTA, scouts, starts working a part time job on Sunday so he cannot spend time with his family. Ten years later he has the money for a second home, has a nicer investment portfolio, but is divorced from his wife and is a stranger to his kids and the community. In this scenario did Joe 1 make a bad/evil decision? I think most of us would say 'YEAH!'

SO, YOU ARE SUGGESTING THAT THE REASONS FOR THE CHANGE IN JOE 1 COULD HAVE BEEN BAD/EVIL, NOT NECESSARILY THE FACT THAT HE DECIDED TO "BETTER HIS LIFE"?

Remember that Joe 1 was content with his life until he started comparing his life to his sister's. A lot of us humans are like that. Why we do that is something for another discussion, and would probably involve a great deal of input from psychologists!

not so easy there, bubba. are rich people who have two or three houses bad or evil?

Unequivocally no. The fact that a person has two or three homes is not an issue. Let's call Joe 2 as the guy who is fortunate enough to be in that position. Is he happy, or is he miserable because his good friend at the country club has four houses? What did his 'success" cost him? His wife? His family? His friends? His self-respect? Maybe it cost him none of those things...

I have friends who have multiple homes, and they are some of the best people I know. Most are talented businessmen, but they are all honorable men and women who are caring and compassionate human beings.

HAVING MONEY IS NOT A CRIME, AND NEITHER IS NOT HAVING MONEY. I WOULD SUGGEST THAT THE MANNER IN WHICH YOU ATTAINED YOUR SUCCESS/MONEY WOULD HAVE A LARGE SAY IN THE TYPE OF PERSON YOU ARE, I.E., IF YOU ARE A MILLIONAIRE BECAUSE YOU SELL DRUGS THAT HURT AND KILL PEOPLE, YOU MAY NOT BE THE GREATEST ASSET TO HUMANITY. IF, HOWEVER, YOU HAVE INVENTED A PRODUCT THAT EMPLOYS 10,000 PEOPLE AND YOU HAVE A CHARITY FOUNDATION THAT DOES GREAT WORK, THEN YOU POSSIBLY WOULD BE AN ASSET TO HUMANITY. IT IS THE GOOD THAT YOU CAN DO FOR HUMANITY AND YOUR MORAL AND ETHICAL

FIBER THAT MAKES UP WHO YOU ARE, NOT THE AMOUNT OF MONEY THAT YOU HAVE.

You do not have to have a lot of money to make society a better place. There are tons of things that does not require money that normal people can do to make this world a better place. For example, what about volunteering at a homeless shelter every month, or working at a community kitchen. That would be of great help!

DR. MIKE IS CORRECT. MONEY IS A GREAT BOON TO MANKIND, CERTAINLY, BUT MAKING LIFE EASIER FOR YOUR FRIENDS, NEIGHBORS, AND THE OTHERS IN YOUR COMMUNITY CAN ALSO BE A GREAT HELP TO THE COMMUNITY.

It does not even have to go that far... if we took care of the members of our own families, correctly and properly, would the world not be a better place?

DID SOMONE JUST BECOME A DEMOCRAT?????

sorry, democrats don't care about families, unless they are immigrants. "it takes a village" remember?

Okay, guys, let's just keep politics out of this. Most politicians do want what is best for the country...they just disagree on how to achieve that. And keep their job, of course. But enough of that. If we, as human beings, truly wanted what is best for this country, there would not be the divisions, the hatred, that we have. I am truly, truly, afraid for what is going to happen to this country. MY COUNTRY!

THAT, I AM AFRAID, IS THE SUBJECT OF ANOTHER DISCUSSION. BUT THE ESSENTIAL CRITERIA THAT WE, AS AMERICANS, HAVE A DUTY TO RESPECT THE RIGHTS OF ALL PEOPLE, EVEN THOSE WITH WHOM WE DISAGREE. THE RESPECT ALSO MEANS THE CONCERN FOR THE WELL-BEING AND WELFARE OF ALL OF OUR NEIGHBORS. THIS IS SOMETHING THAT CAN BE DONE OUTSIDE OF POLITICS AND WOULD PROBABLY BE THE MORE EFFECTIVE USE OF

TIME, TALENTS, AND MONEY. IT STARTS WITH HELPING YOUR FAMILY, YOUR FRIENDS, YOUR NEIGHBORS, YOUR COMMUNITY, YOUR STATE, YOUR NATION, AND THEN CAN EXTEND TO THE WORLD. JUST THINK OF THE POWER OF HOPE AND CONCERN IF EVERY ONE OF US IN THE USA WERE TO DO SOMETHING NICE FOR SOMEONE WE DID NOT KNOW ON A DAILY BASIS. MAYBE HATE WOULD BEGIN TO BE A SMALLER PART OF OUR LIVES, AND OUR POLITICS.

We can only hope, work toward those ideals, and pray that everyone else does too.

that would be wonderful, wouldn't it? all it takes is enough money for all of us to be equal!

It has nothing to do with money, mr. mike. Maybe I am becoming more enlightened as I get older, but people should be respectful, honorable, and honest, no matter what their socio-economic status is. It is, in my opinion, how one feels about himself, or herself, that allows us to be the best possible people we can, thereby being the best friends/neighbor/citizens that we can be. If we all concentrated on being the best people ethically, and morally, that we could be, then our country, and the world, would be in a lot better shape.

THANK YOU, POLLYANNA!

I WOULD HAVE NO ISSUES WITH BEING THE BEST PERSON I CAN BE, IF I HAD ENOUGH MONEY TO DO SO.

i think i can support that idea...

THAT DOES HAVE A BIT OF A NICE RING TO IT; I MUST ADMIT. I COULD GO FOR THAT ALSO.

But, how much is "enough"? Enough to us may not be enough to the Rockefellers or Bill Gates, but it may be enough for the family of five living in a low-income area. But I must admit, I would like a nice ring also.

Guys, you are missing the point...

I AM BEGINNING TO THINK THAT THE SCRIPTURE YOU READ EARLIER SHOULD READ "...FOR THE DISCUSSION OF MONEY IS THE ROOT OF ALL STUPIDITY."

Television

(A medium in which we take mediocracy and inanity, make them a social event, and make the perpetrators rich and famous.)

Author's Note: I like television. There are a number of shows that I would watch even though they may be out of date. I loved the *Twilight Zone* and *Star Trek* among others. Television is an important part of our society, but sometimes it takes itself too seriously. What follows is a discussion of the relative merits of television as it relates to the world in general (the first part), but evolves into a discussion about television when the people discussing the real-world issues cannot agree to what is really critical (second part). Television is important to all the participants, and it is something to which all participants can relate.

michael, i am discouraged.

WHAT SEEMS TO BE THE PROBLEM?

i am worried about the state of the world, the human family, our portfolio, public decency, air pollution, north korea's nuclear capability, our weight, legalizing marijuana, crime, my hair loss, russia, water pollution, unemployment, vladimir putin, president trump, china, democrats, republicans, my hearing loss and...television. in that order.

WELL, LET'S CHAT ABOUT SOMETHING THAT IS WITHIN OUR POWER TO CHANGE OR CORRECT.

GOLLY GEE, MR. WIZARD. THAT RULES OUT JUST ABOUT EVERYTHING!

Wum, quiet. We are trying to have an **INTELLIGENT** conversation. Stay out of it.

i really dislike that guy!

SO, OUT OF YOUR LIST, WE CAN RULE OUT THE FOLLOWING THAT WE CANNOT CHANGE OR CORRECT: NORTH KOREA'S NUCLEAR CAPABILITY, CRIME, OUR HAIR LOSS, RUSSIA, UNEMPLOYMENT, VLADIMIR PUTIN, PRESIDENT TRUMP, CHINA, DEMOCRATS, REPUBLICANS, OR TELEVISION.

what about the others that i mentioned?

TO A CERTAIN EXTENT YOU HAVE SOME ABILITY TO CONTROL ALL OF THOSE REMAINING. FOR EXAMPLE, THE STATE OF THE WORLD. BY LETTING YOUR ELECTED OFFICIALS KNOW HOW YOU FEEL, YOU MAY BE INSTRUMENTAL IN MAKING

CHANGES THAT YOU WOULD LIKE TO SEE MADE. BY BEING A PURE EXAMPLE TO THOSE AROUND YOU OF THE VIRTUES AND IDEALS YOU HOLD MOST DEAR, OTHERS MAY ADMIRE YOUR IDEALS AND WORK FOR THE CHANGE YOU WOULD LIKE TO SEE. THEN, THEORETICALLY, THE STATE OF THE WORLD WOULD CHANGE FOR THE BETTER.

sort of the idea that 'i can't change the world, but i can change myself' idea?

YES, BUT ONE MAN CAN CHANGE THE WORLD. LOOK AT JESUS, OR MOHAMMED, OR BUDDHA, OR EDISON, OR MOTHER TERESA,

OR DONALD TRUMP...

Wum, stay out of this!

I JUST HAVE TO MAKE SURE THAT MY WIT IS BEING RECOGNIZED, AND BRING A LITTLE ENJOYMENT TO THE DISCUSSION.

Trust me, my friend. You are not THAT witty!

OTHER THINGS THAT MAY BE IN THAT CATEGORY ARE THE HUMAN FAMILY, PUBLIC DECENCY, AIR POLLUTION, LEGALIZING MARIJUANA, WATER POLLUTION, AND TELEVISION. THE THINGS THAT ARE LEFT, SUCH AS OUR PORTFOLIO, OUR WEIGHT, AND OUR HEARING LOSS, ARE THINGS THAT WE HAVE COMPLETE CONTROL OVER.

point a – if i had complete control over our portfolio, it would be a lot bigger. point b – if i had complete control of my weight, i would be a lot thinner.

point c — if i had complete control over my hearing loss, i would choose not to lose it!

Point A — we handed control of the portfolio to a professional, and he has done a good job. Point B — If we didn't eat so much, and did some exercise, we would be a lot thinner. It has been our choice. Point C — Hearing Loss is, in part, a function of age. We are getting older, and the alternative to getting older, is not that attractive to me right now!

Well said, Mike.

INDEED, WELL SAID.

okay, since you guys are all against me, let's talk about the one subject that really irritates me... television.

YOU REALIZE THAT YOU CANNOT REALLY DO ANYTHING ABOUT IT, CORRECT?

yes, but we can talk about it in case i ever write a book about it...

MAN, THAT WOULD BE A REALLY DEPRESSING BOOK!

Just ignore him. What about television? You know you have the ability to control the television and its effect on you by choosing, or not choosing, to watch, correct?

yes, i know. but television is so boring, with such boring inept human beings. especially the reality shows...

Such as...

114

big brother, or big mother, whatever it is called... i've never seen it.

NONE OF US HAVE EVER SEEN IT, BUT THERE ARE A LOT OF PEOPLE WHO HAVE, AND THEY MUST LIKE IT. WE MUST BE VERY CAREFUL NOT TO SIMPLY ASSUME THAT OUR LIKES, AND DISLIKES, HAVE TO BE THE LIKES AND DISLIKES OF ALL OF THE TELEVISION VIEWING PUBLIC.

why not?

BECAUSE THERE ARE OVER 311 MILLION PEOPLE IN THIS COUNTRY, AND MOST OF THEM WATCH SOMETHING ON TV! THEY CAN BARELY AGREE ON PICKING A PRESIDENT, LET ALONE SOMETHING AS INCOMPARABLY IMPORTANT AS WHAT TO WATCH ON THE BOOB TUBE!

Mikey, I will handle this...

GEEZ, AND YOU GUYS THINK I AM A WHACKO!

Mikey, go to sleep. Thank you.

THE CRITICAL IDEA IS THAT WITH SO MANY PEOPLE IN OUR COUNTRY...

And so many different points of view on everything from politics to colors of paint.

...WHO HAVE SO MAY DIFFERING VIEWS ON EVERYTHING, THAT IT IS IMPOSSIBLE FOR US TO ASSUME THAT EVERYONE WOULD WANT TO WATCH THE SAME TV PROGRAMS. COLORS OF PAINT, REALLY?

It is the only thing I could think of at the moment. Sorry.

ARE YOU SURE YOU WOULDN'T LIKE TO HAVE ME BACK IN THIS CONVERSATION?

Nope.

NO!

NYET! JUST THOUGHT I WOULD THROW MY 2 CENTS WORTH IN.

can we get back to discussing television? i like tv, but there just does not seem to be much on that interests me, especially with the preponderance of reality shows. what makes it interesting is that because there is a camera there, it is not reality. for example, when any of us know that we are being watched, or interviewed, or whatever, by nature we will act differently than we would if there was no one watching. that, by definition, is not reality.

I can see your point. But 'reality' shows may simply be defined as an 'unscripted' show, as opposed to s a 'scripted' show like NCIS.

but, i have another issue with the term 'reality'. the show about the guy who goes into the wild and is supposed to survive by living off the land...i think it is bear gryllis, or something like that. he has a camera following him, so is that really 'reality'? and, god forbid, if something serious happened, that bear and the cameraman would be out of there so darn fast it would make the olympic 100 meter dash look like a cake-walk!

I THINK THE WHOLE IDEA BEHIND TELEVISION IS TO HELP US ESCAPE FROM OUR REALITY, AND ENJOY OUR EXISTENCE BY SEEING WHAT WE BELIEVE TO BE NORMAL PEOPLE, LIKE OURSELVES, BUT IN FACT ARE REALLY ACTORS BEING PAID TO BE US. THAT IS WHY WE SHOULD EMBRACE OUR LIVES AND THOROUGHLY ENJOY EACH AND EVERY DAY!

i still don't like you!

Is there anything on television that you do like?

sports.

Me too. But I also like some of the shows like "Bull", "NCIS", and "Scorpion".

MY FAVORITE HAS ALWAYS BEEN, AND ALWAYS WILL BE, "THE TWILIGHT ZONE".

WOW! THAT IS OLD! MY FAVORITE IS "MASH".

My favorite was "Barney Miller", and now it is "Judge Judy".

What if we had a show about a guy who was always talking to himself about various subjects, with each of the aspects of his personality being a different person, represented by different people. They could talk about women, and men, and the different things that happen to them during the day. I believe it could really be a hit show, even though most of what happens would be more or less trivial.

sounds interesting...

I think it could work.

THAT COULD BE REALLY SOMETHING!

YEAH! LET'S TALK TO SOMEONE AND DO IT!

GUYS, IT WOULD NOT WORK, AS IT HAS ALREADY BEEN DONE.

You mean to tell me that there was a television program about people discussing the trivial, mundane things of life? And each of the personalities on the show had differing perspectives which guided their thoughts and actions? And they interacted as if they were real people?

YES. THE SHOW WAS "SEINFELD".

College Sports

(College sports, professional sports – what is the difference?)

Author's Note: As noted above, I love sports, including college sports. In watching the changes that have happened to college sports over the past 30 years, it has come to my attention that some college sports act as a feeding system to the professional sporting business. This discussion that follows is an attempt to bring to light, hopefully in a humorous fashion, the changes that have occurred in the realm of college athletics. I hope you enjoy the give and take of the discussion.

I have heard that there is a move afoot to start paying collegiate basketball players, instead of having them receive scholarships.

I KNOW THERE HAS BEEN A GREAT DEAL OF DISCUSSION ABOUT THAT IDEA, BUT IT NEVER SEEMS TO GET OFF THE GROUND.

What do you think if the idea?

AT HEART, I AM AGAINST THE IDEA. IT SEEMS TO ME THAT THE IDEA OF BEING A PROFESSIONAL, I.E., BEING PAID TO PLAY A SPORT IS AGAINST THE WHOLE IDEA OF 'STUDENT' ATHLETES. IT JUST SEEMS WRONG.

it is all just hogwash. these guys and girls get paid anyway.

Not in cash. They receive tuition, books, a place to live and some meals. That is it.

boy, are you naïve! ever heard of boosters?

Yes, I have, and you are right. There are plenty of boosters, and some of them even make mistakes...

it is still just hogwash. they get privileges above and beyond what you have stated, and generally they do not go to 'meaningful' classes, like normal students.

They go to class...

'how to dribble a basketball through a zone press' is hardly a match for 'advanced calculus and analytical geometry'.

MR. MIKE, YOU ARE REALLY DOWN ON THESE PEOPLE, AREN'T YOU? WHAT TURNED YOU INTO SUCH A GRUMP ABOUT THIS SUBJECT?

Because it is a waste of time, talent, and taxpayer money to fund college sports programs when few, if any, make positive contributions to the university that they attend.

I disagree. The universities receive, for the most part, positive feedback for successful athletic programs, and the money they make from men's basketball and football help also. That allows a lot more athletes in non-traditional sports to have the college experience also.

so, if what you are saying is true, then why not pay all athletes, regardless of sport? i mean, why not pay the track athlete as well as the basketball athlete? and, if we are going to pay them, are they students or employees of the university, and do they have to attend classes, or just show up for work, i.e., practice and games?

I AM NOT SURE THERE IS AN ANSWER TO THAT ONE. WHAT WOULD YOU SUGGEST?

i think i would be in favor of just having them be employees of the university. they could get a wage, have some benefits like health insurance, 401k's, etc. i am not sure how that would work out with vacation days, sick days, performance reviews, etc.

AND JUST THINK OF HOW MUCH MONEY THE SCHOOL WOULD SAVE BY NOT HAVING TO BUY LETTERPERSON SWEATERS OR JACKETS. THEY COULD REPLACE THE LETTERPERSON SWEATERS/JACKETS WITH T-SHIRTS THAT SAY "BASKETBALL EMPLOYEE", "FOOTBALL EMPLOYEE" OR WHATEVER "EMPLOYEE". THEY COULD HAVE THE STUDENT ATHLETES...I AM SORRY. NOT STUDENT ATHLETES BUT **EMPLOYEE ATHLETES.** IT DOES HAVE A NICE SOUND TO IT.

i like it!

It does have a nice ring to it, kind of like 'stupendously mediocre' or 'new and improved'!

MIKE, I HAVE TO ADMIT IT – SARCASM IS NOT YOUR STRONG SUIT.

WELL, THE TWO OF YOU ARE THE SAME PERSON.

can we get back to the discussion at hand? thank you. if our employee athlete is just that, what would be the payment structure? i personally think that they should be paid out of the athletic department budget, as should all employees of the athletic department, and they should be paid on performance, like the coaches.

SHOULD THEY GET THE SAME SALARY AS OTHER UNIVERSITY EMPLOYEES, SUCH AS A PROFESSOR? I MEAN, UNIVERSITIES PAY A TENURED PROFESSOR $100,000 PER YEAR, BUT A SUCCESSFUL BASKETBALL COACH CAN MAKE $300.000 BASE SALARY WITH BONUSES AND OUTSIDE DEALS THAT CAN MEAN AN ADDITIONAL FOUR TO FIVE MILLION. SO, HOW MUCH ARE YOU GOING TO PAY THE EMPLOYEE ATHLETE?

GEEZ, I SHOULD HAVE BEEN A BASKETBALL COACH...

Maybe we are looking at this incorrectly. Since we now have employee athletes, why not be like the coaches and allow the school, not the coaches, to 'sell' the right to wear and advertise from athletic companies, thereby allowing the players to reap some of the rewards that the coaches do. You could even go one step further and suggest that it is the athletic department that should be doing the 'selling', thereby ensuring that all employee athletes would benefit from the athletic department's success.

Mike, I think you are onto something. If the school did the selling, the school could then establish a value for the employee athlete in each sport. Then, by paying a 'set' amount the school could establish a reserve fund for athletic success (bonuses) to be distributed at the end of the season/academic cycle, based upon the university president and the board of governors' joint decision. Once the athletic departments have taken their share/bonuses, the balance would be back in the hands of the university to improve the salaries of the people who are the reason for the university in the first place, the professors.

Thanks, Dr, Mike.

THAT WOULD OPEN UP COLLEGE ATHLETICS TO BIDDING WARS AND THE AXIOM THAT THE 'RICH GET RICHER, AND THE POOR GET POORER'.

isn't that what we have now? look at college football for example. unless you are in a 'power 5' conference, the chances are very slim that you can get into the college playoffs. the university of central florida is a perfect example. ucf went undefeated and played, and beat, the team that beat both schools that played for the "national championship", auburn. auburn beat both georgia and alabama during the

123

regular season, but georgia and alabama got into the playoff, and ucf did not. go figure.

THAT IS A TOPIC FOR A LENGTHY DISCUSSION AT SOME OTHER TIME.

i understand that, but when the rich are getting richer by having an advantage simply because of the conference in which they play is 'supposedly better' then the poor are going to continue to become poorer until they join one of the power 5 conferences. that is not right, especially when a lot of the power 5 conferences have less than mediocre teams. no wonder you only have one loss if you play teams that consistently are not very good, and lose lots of games.

I agree with the idea, but once again that is a topic for another time.

MAYBE WE CAN DISCUSS IT AT FURTHER LENGTH IN THE FUTURE IF THINGS DO NOT CHANGE IN THE NEAR FUTURE.

MAYBE WE COULD DISCUSS IT IN THE NEXT BOOK!

is he still here?

But getting back to the discussion of paying college athletes, if that were to happen wouldn't that simply divide the colleges into the 'haves' and the 'have nots', and further the disruption of college athletics?

WE ALREADY HAVE THAT. YOU HAVE THE NCAA AND THE NAIA, ALONG WITH MULTIPLE DIVISIONS IN EACH OF THE AREAS. IN THE NCAA YOU HAVE THE DIVISION 1 SCHOOLS, THE DIVISION 2 SCHOOLS, AND THE DIVISION 3 SCHOOLS, AND THAT IS JUST IN FOOTBALL. THEN YOU HAVE SOME

DIVISION 1 SCHOOLS IN BASKETBALL THAT DO NOT HAVE A FOOTBALL PROGRAM. THEN YOU ALSO HAVE SCHOOLS THAT DO NOT GIVE SCHOLARSHIPS TO ATHLETES, AND THEY PLAY FOR THE 'LOVE OF THE GAME' OR TO HAVE FUN DATING, WHATEVER THE CASE MAY BE.

That is true. A friend of ours went to s small college in Ohio and was on the wrestling team for four years. I do not think he had a scholarship, but he did it just to compete because he loved wrestling.

Maybe we should just make the premise that college athletes should only be paid at certain schools, of the school's choice, and in certain sports...

but they are getting paid! if they have a scholarship for tuition, books, room and board, and meals that is payment. what they do with that payment is part of the problem and the issue. for example, if i have a scholarship to play football and yet all i do is go to practice and mess around and do not go to any 'meaningful' classes, and do not make it as a professional football player, what good was the payment that i received, i.e., tuition, books, etc.?

BUT THAT IS A PERSONAL ISSUE WITH EVERY PERSON THAT ACCEPTS A SCHOLARSHIP. MANY STUDENT ATHLETES GO TO SCHOOLS ON SCHOLARSHIP WITH THE GOAL OF PERHAPS BECOMING A PRO. BUT MANY REALIZE THAT A.) THEY DO NOT HAVE THE TALENT TO BE A PRO; B.) THEY MAY HAVE THE TALENT, BUT THEIR WORK ETHIC HINDERS THEIR DEVELOPMENT; C.) THEY REALIZE THAT THE LIFE OF A PRO IS NOT WHAT THEY WANT; OR D.) THEY ARE INJURED AND CAN NO LONGER PLAY TO THE LEVEL REQUIRED. THESE ARE THE STUDENT ATHLETES THAT DO GO TO CLASS AND TAKE ADVANTAGE OF THE OPPORTUNITY THAT THEY HAVE TO

BETTER THEIR LIVES. THAT IS ADMIRABLE AND WORTHY OF PRAISE. IT IS ALSO ADMIRABLE AND PRAISEWORTHY TO MENTION KIDS WHO DO NOT HAVE SCHOLARSHIPS BUT PERSEVERE AND MAKE A BETTER LIFE FOR THEMSELVES. ONCE AGAIN, THAT IS A PERSONAL ISSUE, AND A PERSONAL CHOICE.

I am glad of the choices we made.

In September, 2019, Governor Newsom of California signed into law a bill that would allow athletes to profit from their talents and the use of their likenesses, and eleven other states are considering similar laws. I think that in the near future we will see some changes in college sports, especially if other states join California.

When does that law become effective?

Not until 2023. By then everything will be worked out.

Wow!

IT WILL BE INTERESTING TO SEE THE EFFECT ON COLLEGE SPORTS, THE NCAA, AND RECRUITING WHEN IT HAPPENS. I THINK WE WILL SEE A LOT OF CHANGES OVER THE NEXT FEW YEARS. MAYBE WE SHOULD HAVE BEEN A PROFESSIONAL ATHLETE

WHY? WHAT DOES A PROFESSIONAL ATHLETE HAVE THAT WE DON'T? I COULD HAVE BEEN A PROFESSIONAL ATHLETE, BUT I CHOSE A DIFFERENT PATH. AM I A FAILURE? I THINK NOT.

WUM IS CORRECT. THERE ARE TONS OF REASONS WHY PEOPLE FAIL TO BECOME PROFESSIONAL ATHLETES. IN OUR CASE IT MAY HAVE BEEN THAT WE WERE TOO SMALL, TOO STUPID, TOO AFRAID, ETC.

i vote for wum being the stupid one.

I think that may be 100% correct.

HE GETS MY VOTE!

Mine too!

WHAT A MORON!!!!!!!!!!!!!!!!!!

TO QUOTE JAMES CAAN FROM THE MOVIE "*EL DORADO*" -"I HAVE A HOST OF FRIENDS!"

Genealogy

("He is a self-made man and worships his creator." – Henry Clapp)

Author's Note: We all wonder who we really are, and where we came from. Genealogy can help with that. In our little discussion here, some may not be as free to admit where the genealogy helps, or hurts. The simple fact is that there are no 100% bloodlines, which means we literally are all related.

I just got my DNA results back.

oh, please tell me we are not from cleveland.

DNA results do not go with exact cities. What is wrong with Cleveland anyway?

have you ever lived there?

WE HAVE ALL LIVED THERE, YOU TWIT!

MIKEY, PLAY NICE. AS I RECALL WE ALL HAD A VERY NICE TIME IN CLEVELAND. IT REALLY IS A BEAUTIFUL CITY...

IF YOU LIKE RIVERS AND LAKES THAT CATCH ON FIRE!

That, I believe was a one-time situation, and it has not happened again. Cleveland has some of the nicest suburbs, with some beautiful homes, and it is a very nice place to live. I would not mind living there again...

no!

NOT A CHANCE IN HECK!

I would not think that would be a particularly good thing to do for a number of reasons. (1) It is far away from all of your children; (2) Would you rather live in the climate of SoCal or the climate of Cleveland. I think SoCal makes more sense...

I KNOW IT MAKES MORE SENSE TO LIVE IN SOCAL...THAT IS WHY WE HAVE SO MANY PEOPLE HERE!!!!!!!!!!

...and (3) Our beautiful, wonderful Patti would probably divorce you if you wanted to move to Cleveland.

IF SHE DIVORCES YOU, I AM OUTTA HERE!

me too!

SOMETHING, I THINK, WE CAN FINALLY AGREE UPON!

I MUST ADMIT, BUT WUM, MIKEY, AND MR. MIKE DO HAVE A POINT.

Do not forget about me. I would go with the group, strictly upon statistical grounds, of course.

OF COURSE.

Guys, do not worry! It is not going to happen. I am NOT moving to Cleveland... but on the other hand, would it be so bad if it were just me, without the rest of you hanging around?

Did he really just say that?

OH BROTHER! YOU HAVE JUST STEPPED OVER THE LINE, BUBBA!

HE MAY NOT LIKE YOU GUYS, BUT HE HAS TO LIKE ME. I AM THE FUN ONE, AND WE ALL LIKE TO HAVE FUN. SO, IT MUST BE YOU GUYS THAT HE DOESN'T WANT AROUND!

No, maybe it is all of you.

EVEN ME? HOW CAN YO SAY THAT? I AM THE ONE THAT ALLOWED YOU TO HAVE A PERSONALITY. THANKS A LOT!

FELLAS, DO NOT WORRY. MIKE, EVEN WITH HIS "SUPERIOR CAPACITIES" (WINK, WINK), COULD NOT SURVIVE WITHOUT

US. AND BESIDES, TRUTH BE KNOWN, ALL OF US ARE A PART OF THE SAME PERSON, AND WE COME OUT AT DIFFERENT TIMES. WE ARE ALL NEEDED, RIGHT MIKE?

Yes! Of course. I was just messing with you. Now, can we get back to our DNA results?

YES.

YOU BETCHA!

can we leave wum out of this conversation?

No, because this affects us all. We will simply ask him to lessen his input by not making stupid jokes or comments.

WOW! HE WON'T BE ABLE TO SAY A WORD! LOVE IT!

THAT HURTS.

AHAH. YOU CAN DISH IT OUT BUT YOU CAN'T TAKE IT!

Can we get back to DNA results, please?

Yes, that is a great idea.

Our DNA came back 49% Great Britain, 42% Scandinavia, 4% Ireland, 1% European Jewish, and 4% Other areas, such as Eastern Europe, Western Europe, Western Russia, Greece, and Cleveland.

what???

Just kidding about the Cleveland part. So, it basically supports what we have known all along.

DOES THAT SURPRISE YOU? I MEAN, YOU HAVE HAD YOUR GENEALOGY BACK PRETTY FAR FOR A LONG TIME.

Yes, I know that. But it does bring up a couple of questions.

like what?

I never knew I was part Irish. Doesn't that scare you?

THE IRISH ARE GOOD PEOPLE! AND THAT MAY EXPLAIN WHY POTATOES HAVE BEEN SUCH A BIG PART OF YOUR LIFE.

I CAN'T WAIT TO HEAR THIS ONE.

WE WERE BORN IN IDAHO, WHOSE MOTTO SHOULD BE 'HAVE A SPUD, BUD', AND ONE SUMMER WE WORKED FOR A POTATO FARMER MOVING IRRIGATION PIPE IN MICHIGAN WHILE IN HIGH SCHOOL IN INDIANA! AND, WE LOVE MASHED POTATOES, AS LONG AS THEY ARE A BIT LUMPY, AND BAKED POTATOES, AND FRENCH FRIES, AND POTATOES AND GRAVY...

I HATE TO SAY THIS, BUT WUM HAS MADE SOME GOOD ARGUMENTS.

"have a spud, bud????????"

Of course, the Irish are good people, but it was just a bit of a shock to have part of my DNA from there.

There may be some good reasons for this. The 49% from Great Britain, I am sure, includes Wales, and we know that a lot of our people come from Wales. Ireland is, of course, an island which is on the Western coast of Great Britain, and Wales is the closest part of the island of Great Britain to Ireland. Maybe there was a little bit of close quarter action which resulted in some Irish DNA being deposited in our bloodline.

Well, that may be true. I am wondering if there is any reason to trust any DNA sample.

Why would you say that?

Let's say that we humans have been around for, oh, let's say six thousand years. In all this time there have been interactions with virtually all peoples everywhere in the world. Look at the conquests that various peoples have made through history, such as the Vikings, the Mongols, the Arabs — virtually every country/region has been overrun by an 'enemy', which I am sure has contributed to introducing different DNA into the local mixture. If this trend continues, especially in our modern era of easy travel, and easy everything else, we all may end up with the same DNA anyway.

IS THAT SUCH A BAD THING? MAYBE IT WOULD THEN CONVINCE PEOPLE TO EXAMINE THEIR OWN IDEAS ABOUT OTHER PEOPLE AND OTHER CULTURES, SIMPLY BECAUSE WE WOULD ALL HAVE THE SAME BASIC DNA, I.E., WE ARE ALL RELATED.

But if we have to wait until we all have the same DNA just to love and appreciate other people, then we have not learned the lessons from history that we should have. We have six thousand years of human interaction, and it is a story of war, genocide, and greed. Aside from a few humans like Jesus, Buddah, and others, the main approach of human history has been to overpower, enslave, and destroy those who have something we want, or are different, in whatever way than we are.

WE COULD GO INTO AN INFINITE AND NEVER-ENDING DEBATE AS TO WHY THESE THINGS HAPPEN, BUT THIS IS NEITHER THE TIME NOR PLACE TO DO SO. THE ABILITY OF HUMANS TO ADAPT TO THEIR ENVIRONMENTS IS A FASCINATING STUDY, AS ARE THE CULTURAL TRADITIONS OF ALL HUMANS.

I BELIEVE THAT GOD INTENDED FOR US HUMANS TO GET ALONG, AND HE GAVE US WAYS TO DO SO – A CONSCIENCE, THE TEACHINGS OF GREAT MEN, AND THE ABILITY TO MAKE CHOICES, ETC. OUR PROBLEM IS THAT TOO MANY HUMANS CHOOSE WHAT IS EASIEST, OR BEST FOR THEM, REGARDLESS OF WHAT IS RIGHT OR APPROPRIATE.

No matter what our DNA says, it all comes down to ethics, morals, law, and choice, and the effect on others of our course of action, and whether or not what the ethics or morals or law or choices is better for the individual or group of individuals, i.e., whether it be a culture or a nation, or for the neighboring culture or nation. Is that what you are saying?

what are you talking about?

It is the age-old question of nurture versus nature…

I JUST CHECKED THE RESULTS FROM LAST NIGHT... NURTURE WON, 47-46.

WHY DO WE LET HIM SPEAK? YES, THAT IS CORRECT. WHAT THEN MAKES THE DISCUSSION EVEN MORE INTERESTING IS THE EXTENT TO WHICH THERE ARE COMMONALITIES BETWEEN THE ETHICS, MORALS, AND LAWS OF DIFFERENT SOCIETIES, AND THE LIBERALITY INHERENT IN THOSE MORALS, ETHICS, AND LAWS. FOR EXAMPLE, IF I HAVE A SOCIETY IN WHICH YO-YOS (YOYOFREELAND) ARE FORBIDDEN, WHAT HAPPENS WHEN A VISITOR FROM ANOTHER SOCIETY (YOYOLAND) VISITS, AND IS PLAYING WITH A YO-YO IN A PUBLIC PLACE? IS THE PERSON TO BE TAKEN AND IMPRISONED, OR IS HIS/HER YO-YO SIMPLY TO BE TAKEN AND IMPOUNDED OR DESTROYED? THE VISITING FAMILY MAY LEAVE AND WILL PROBABLY NEVER AGAIN COME TO YOYOFREELAND, AND WILL PROBABLY NOT SPEAK HIGHLY OF THEIR VISIT. WILL THE CITIZENS OF YOYOLAND THEN SUGGEST THAT THEIR

RIGHT TO YO-YO WAS DENIED, AND THEN ACT TO ATTEMPT TO CHANGE THE LAW OF YOYOFREELAND TO THEIR LIKING? THEN, IF THOSE EFFORTS FAIL THEM, WILL THE CITIZENS OF YOYOLAND DECLARE WAR UPON THE CITIZENS OF YOYOFREELAND AND ATTEMPT TO FORCE THEM TO ALLOW YOYO PLAYING? IS THAT WHAT THE SIX THOUSAND YEARS OF HUMAN HISTORY HAS BROUGHT US TO?

I think your example may be a little far-fetched, don't you think?

I AGREE. I CAN'T SEE ANYONE GOING TO WAR OVER YO-YO'S. SOCCER GAMES, YES, BUT YO-YO'S? NOT A CHANCE.

YET IN THE HISTORY OF HUMAN DEVELOPMENT, WARS AND BATTLES HAVE OCCURRED FOR LESSER REASONS.

If we all had the same ethics, morals, and laws — that would help would it not?

DID IT SOLVE THE ISSUES THAT BECAME THE REVOLUTIONARY WAR? PEOPLE PROCESS THINGS DIFFERENTLY, AND EVEN IN OUR GREAT LAND, THERE ARE VAST DIVISIONS OVER WHAT IS ETHICAL, WHAT IS MORAL, AND WHAT CONSTITUTES THE 'COMMON GOOD'.

Boy, isn't that the truth! Look at smoking. I do not think I have ever met someone who did not wish they had never smoked, yet I have met plenty of them that wished they had never started the habit. Yet, we know it is harmful, but it is legal. Go figure.

Maybe, just maybe, there is something in the DNA that causes more people to be susceptible to things like that while other peoples' DNA doesn't. I am not quite sure that we understand the full impact of DNA on actions...the question of nurture versus nature is still relevant.

I HAVE A SOLUTION.

here it comes...

MAKE ME THE KING OF THE WORLD, AND ALL PROBLEMS WILL CEASE. SO AS LONG AS EVERYONE WILL DO WHAT I WANT THEM TO, THE PROBLEM IS SOLVED. CORRECT?

what if the people did not want to do what you wanted them to?

THAT IS IRRELEVANT. THE PEOPLE WOULD LOVE ME SO MUCH THAT THEY WOULD AUTOMATICALLY DO EVERYTHING THAT I WOULD ASK. I WOULD BE SUCH A GREAT KING THAT THERE WOULD NEVER, EVER, BE ANYONE NOT DOING WHAT I ASKED.

I DO NOT THINK THAT WOULD WORK.

Me either.

WHY NOT?

YOU ARE TALKING ABOUT TAKING THE ABILITY TO CHOOSE AWAY FROM PEOPLE, AND THAT IS NOT A GOOD THING. WHY WOULD ANYONE WANT TO DO ONLY WHAT YOU SAID?

BECAUSE THAT WOULD BE THE BEST FOR THEM! ALL THE DECISIONS WOULD BE MADE FOR THEM, AND THERE WOULD NOT BE ANY PROBLEMS. EVERYONE WOULD BE HAPPY WITH PEACEFUL LIVES. SORT OF LIKE 'PLEASANTVILLE'!

OKAY, LET US TEST YOUR THEORY. WUM WANTS US TO FOLLOW HIS DIRECTION AND DO EVERYTHING HE WANTS US TO DO. MIKEY, HOW DO YOU VOTE?

LET ME PUT IT THIS WAY – NOT FOR ALL OF THE TEA IN CHINA, ALL THE SNOW IN SIBERIA, THE TWIZZLERS AND ALL THE CHOCOLATES IN THE WORLD OR THE GOLD IN...

HOW DO YOU VOTE?

I VOTE 'NO'.

Dr. Mike, how do you vote?

After much deliberation and discussions with my constituencies, I vote 'no' also.

I AM GOING TO LOSE, AREN'T I?

TOO CLOSE TO CALL. MIKE, HOW ABOUT YOU?

I believe it is the best interest of my genealogical conscience to vote 'no'.

I THOUGHT YOU LIKED ME?

I do. I just think you would make a lousy dictator.

MR. MIKE, WHAT DO YOU THINK? HOW WOULD YOUR VOTE GO, ALTHOUGH I THINK I KNOW.

mr. mike would definitely say nay.

I THOUGHT SO. WELL, WUM, RIGHT NOW YOU ARE LOSING 4-0. I WOULD SUSPECT THAT YOU WOULD VOTE FOR YOURSELF, SO I AM GOING TO SUGGEST THAT THE TALLY IS NOW 4-1. TO CLOSE THE POLLS, I WOULD HAVE TO SAY THAT I, ON THE STRENGTH OF WHAT I KNOW OF ALL OF US, AND THE DEFINITE FEELINGS THAT I HAVE FOR EACH OF YOU, I WOULD VOTE 'NO' ALSO. SO, THE FINAL TALLY IS 5-1.

NO, NOT REALLY. I WOULD N'T VOTE FOR MYSELF EITHER, SO THE FINAL TALLY WOULD BE 6-0.

Wow! I am shocked. I thought for sure that you would vote for yourself.

NOT REALLY. I KNOW THAT DEPRIVING PEOPLE OF THE RIGHT TO CHOOSE IS AGAINST OUR DNA AS HUMAN BEINGS, AS PROVEN IN A SETTING IN THE DISTANT PAST. A PERVEYOR OF UNTRUTH AND DICTATORIAL PRACTICES TRIED TO SUGGEST THAT THAT WAS THE BEST WAY TO BE GOOD PEOPLE.

OH, WHERE WAS THAT?

IN THE PREMORTAL LIFE.

And the purveyor was...

LUCIFER, WHO BECAME SATAN. HE HAS BEEN TRYING TO GET US TO DO BAD THINGS EVER SINCE!

Men

("As long as you know men are like children,
you know everything!" – Coco Chanel)

Author's Note: We had a discussion on 'Women', it is only fair to
have a discussion on 'Men'. Sometimes I have seen men do weird
things that has made me wonder 'what were they thinking?' It is
only fair that we give the men an equal discussion. I hope you enjoy
this dialogue.

Michael, are women different from men?

HOW LONG HAVE YOU BEEN MARRIED?

You know the answer to that. About forty-five years.

ABOUT?

HOW DID WE EVER HAVE KIDS?

I know the "difference" between men and women, yes. It just seems that men and women are the same species, but different — like beautiful lionesses and fat, slothful lions.

GOOD ANALOGY, BUT I AM NOT SURE WHAT YOU ARE GETTING AT.

Well, I am not quite sure what I mean. Sometimes I wonder if there is a real difference in the way men and women act or respond to certain things, and are the differences something that is in the natures of the beast, or what?

i thought we already talked about this nature versus nurture idea?

WE DID, BUT NOT IN ITS TOTALITY.

Yes, the 'totality', if you will, would suggest that there is an immeasurable difference between the thoughts of women and the thoughts of men, given the NATURE of the beasts. But then you factor in the differences is the nurture part, i.e., making allowances for the differences in culture, religion, political standing and practices, etc. It leads to a tremendous amount of support for the overriding assumption that to know, with some sort of accuracy or precision, the differences between men and women as a whole, is virtually impossible. But the ability to know the differences between an individual man and an individual woman may be easier to acknowledge and fathom the longer that an individual man and an individual woman were together.

YOU ARE SAYING THAT IN ORDER TO UNDERSTAND THE DIFFERENCES BETWEEN MAN AND WOMAN, IT WILL TAKE LOTS OF TIME STUDYING THE DIFFERENCES AND BEING WITH THEM, IN ORDER TO UNDERSTAND OUR DIFFERENCES?

MIKEY, MIKEY, MIKEY...DON'T WORRY ABOUT IT! WHAT WOMAN WOULD BE ATTRACTED TO YOU ANYWAY!

Dr. Mike, just curious. In your valued and scientific approach to the world, how much time does it take, for the average male, to understand an average woman?

For the average male of the species, given his tendency to fixate on things other than the female of the species, about 457.29 years. Give or take a few decades depending upon how "enlightened" or "unenlightened" he is.

And the average life span of the average male these days?

Depending, of course upon the numerous variables that exist in the differing parts of our human globe, the lifespan today of the male could range from 70 to 95, depending upon the circumstances...

The point being that if it takes a man 460 years...

457.29 to be exact...

Okay. 457.29. The point is that you are suggesting that even if a man lives less than 457.29 years, he will **NEVER** understand a woman. Correct?

Well, Mike, you still have to factor in the obvious fact that until a boy reaches puberty, he really has no interest in girls or women, except Mom, of course. Therefore, his attention is drawn to simple things that he CAN understand such as sports, or comic books, or ancient Greek and Roman culture. Then the actuality of the lifespan range in which he may understand women shrinks from the '70 to 95' range to the '58 to 83' assuming that puberty is reached somewhere around the 12-year-old phase.

IF I MAY, DR. MIKE, MAKE A SLIGHT INPUT TO YOUR LOGIC. EVEN AT PUBERTY, THE THOUGHTS A BOY HAS DO NOT REALLY CLIMB TO THE THRESHOLD OF TRYING TO "UNDERSTAND" WOMEN FOR THE VERY SIMPLE REASON THAT THEY ARE STILL TRYING TO FIGURE OUT THEIR OWN PLACE AND IDENTITY, LET ALONE ATTEMPTING TO UNDERSTAND GIRLS AND WOMEN.

It sounds as if you have had some of those issues in your own life.

YES, WE HAVE.

Oops. I forgot for a moment. Yes, we have. I can truthfully say that, without a doubt, you are correct in your input. A boy never really begins to understand women until he seriously considers who he wants to be with for the balance of his life. Then he will start to seriously consider an attempt to understand what it is that he is looking for, and then up to that point. Now, let's assume that our male begins to think of those things in his mid-twenties, let's say 25. That would suggest that our friend has lost an additional 13 years (from 12 to 25) where in the primary focus was not to understand women, but to go to college or get a job or play video games or whatever. This shrinks the understanding women range from the '58 to 83' range down to '45 to 70' range in years to understand women.

Geez, that is not a lot of time...

WE ARE NEVER GOING TO UNDERSTAND THEM IN THIS LIFE, SO I VOTE WE JUST IGNORE THEM, HAVE FUN, AND GO OUR MERRY LITTLE WAY.

WUM, THAT IS NOT EVEN REMOTELY POSSIBLE.

WHY?

YOU ARE MARRIED, MORON. AND I MIGHT ADD TO THE MOST WONDERFUL WOMAN IN THE WORLD.

SO, IF SHE IS THE 'MOST WONDERFUL WOMAN IN THE WORLD', WHY DID SHE PICK US?

THAT IS A VERY GOOD QUESTION, AND ONE THAT WE ALL HAVE BEEN ASKING. I THINK SHE SAW SOMETHING IN ALL OF US THAT ATTRACTS GREATNESS.

Or maybe intense mediocrity that she believed she could change...

IT WAS THE SEX!

WHO ARE YOU??????????

YOU CAN CALL ME MICKY. I AM THE PART OF OUR PERSON THAT HARBORS THE DEEP, DARK SECRETS OF THE MIND, AND BODY. I AM THE PERSONA THAT NO ONE EVER WANTS TO TALK TO IN POLITE SOCIETY.

I HAD A FEELING THAT YOU WERE GOING TO SHOW UP.

As the resident dominant personality in this mind-set, I must admit that I did not know you existed.

THAT IS BECAUSE YOU NEVER WANTED TO ACKOWLEDGE THAT THERE ARE DEEP, DARK SECRETS IN YOUR MIND.

Oh, I acknowledge them, but I did not want to give them a front row seat, as it were, to my thoughts and actions.

WHY NOT?

If they are dark secrets, I do not wish them to be a part of my life and actions. I do believe in right and wrong, and there are a number of things that qualify as being inappropriate. Those things, I try to ignore, and not do.

DO YOU THINK ABOUT SEX?

WE ARE A MAN...WHAT ELSE ARE WE GOING TO THINK ABOUT?

WUM, YOU ARE NOT HELPING.

Alright, I think I see where you are going with this. Yes, I think about s-e-x. Always have, even when I wasn't having s-e-x, I would still think about it. We all know that. We enjoy s-e-x, have always enjoyed s-e-x, and I think we always will. Is there something deep and dark about that?

DO YOU THINK ABOUT SEX WITH WOMEN OTHER THAN YOUR WIFE?

No.

WHY NOT?

Because I believe that sex is something that should be enjoyed in the sanctity of the marriage bed. I believe that the love between a man and a woman is a sacred trust, and should not be defiled.

HAVE YOU EVER BEEN UNFAITHFUL TO YOUR WIFE?

I plead the fifth amendment.

AHAH! SO, YOU HAVE!

*THE FIFTH AMENDMENT ONLY SUGGESTS THAT THE PERSON
PLEADING THE FIFTH REFUSES TO ANSWER THE QUESTION,
AND GUILT OR INNOCENCE SHOULD NOT BE ASSUMED SIMPLY
BECAUSE THE PERSON WANTS TO IGNORE THE QUESTION!*

Thank you, Michael. Micky, what are the secrets that you so egregiously make sure stay hidden?

THERE IS NOTHING HORRIBLE. I MEAN, IT IS NOT LIKE YOU HAVE MURDERED SOMEONE AND BURIED THE BODY. IT IS JUST THAT YOU WANT THE WORLD TO THINK VERY HIGHLY OF YOU, AND IN YOUR MIND, YOU HAVE DIFFERENT MEMORIES AND THOUGHTS THAT MAY SHOW YOU TO BE A DIFERENT PERSON THAN YOU ARE TO PEOPLE AROUND YOU, THAT IS ALL.

But, if I never act on those thoughts, am I being that sort of person that you do not want me to be? "What ere thou art, act well thy part" is still a good motto, correct?

WELL, YES...

And the motto states "What ere thou art, **ACT** well thy part" (William Shakespeare), not "What ere thou art, THINK well thy part", correct?

WELL, YES...

What is truly important in our life is what we are, not what we think. Thoughts are important as they lead to action, but action is the critical item in our lives because what we do reflects on what we think, believe, and believe strongly enough to act upon those ideas. That is what makes a man, and a good man is guided by good thoughts, thereby creating good actions.

And quite frankly, the same thing can be said for the female of the species. Good thoughts lead to good actions which lead to good women.

MAYBE THE DIFFERENCES BETWEEN MEN AND WOMEN ISN'T SO GREAT AS WE THINK...MAYBE IT IS SIMPLY THE UNDERLYING GOODNESS/MORALITY THAT SHOULD EXIST IN OUR LIVES.

I AGREE. I WILL NOW GO BACK INTO HIDING AND BE THE KEEPER OF ALL THE DEEP, DARK SECRETS. JUST TRY NOT TO HAVE ANY MORE...I KIND OF WOULD LIKE A VACATION.

Deal. Thanks, Micky. You have provided me with insights into my character that I should have realized years ago. You are an important part of us.

BUT WE ALL MUST REMEMBER THAT AS THOUGHT CAN LEAD TO ACTION, THEREFORE WE NEED TO BE CAREFUL ABOUT OUR THOUGHTS, AND WHERE THEY CAN LEAD.

True. We do need to be careful about what thoughts we let into our mind. One can never tell where those thoughts will lead us.

NOW THAT THAT IS SETTLED, CAN WE GO BACK TO THINKING ABOUT SEX?

Books

("Outside of a dog, a book is man's best friend.
Inside of a dog, it's too dark to read."
Attributed to Groucho Marx)

Author's Note: This discussion is the result of having a recent experience at a book store, and then goes into a discussion of some of my favorite books, and why they are my favorites. It gives you a little sampling of my taste in literature, and also gives an insight into the basis of my sense of humor.

I AM UPSET!

What is going on, Mikey?

I BOUGHT A BOOK AT A BOOKSTORE. IT WAS PRICED AS A NEW BOOK, AND I PAID THE FULL PRICE. I NOTICED THAT WHILE I WAS READING IT, THERE WERE ABOUT 15 PAGES WITH THE CORNER TURNED DOWN THROUGHOUT THE BOOK. THE LAST ONE BEING RIGHT BEFORE THE LAST CHAPTER. OBVIOUSLY, SOMEONE FROM THE BOOKSTORE TOOK THE BOOK, READ IT, AND THEN PLACED IT BACK ON THE SHELF AS A NEW BOOK WHEN THEY WERE FINISHED WITH IT. IT IRRITATED ME, GREATLY!

Did you talk to the bookstore about it?

YES, AND THEY APOLOGIZED PROFUSELY, AND OFFERED TO REPLACE THE BOOK WITH A NEW ONE. WHAT I REALLY WANTED WAS A RETURN OF SOME OF MY FUNDS FOR PAYING NEW PRICE FOR A USED BOOK.

I WAS MONITORING THIS WHEN IT HAPPENED, AND I BELIEVE THAT THEY DID OFFER YOU PARTIAL REPAYMENT, DID THEY NOT?

YES, THEY DID, BUT IT WAS NOT QUITE AS MUCH AS THE DIFFERENCE BETWEEN A NEW AND A USED BOOK.

BUT IT WAS SOMETHING THAT THEY OFFERED, AND YOU DECIDED AGAINST IT, CORRECT?

YES, BECAUSE I BUY A LOT OF BOOKS THERE, AND I FELT I RAISED A BIG ENOUGH STINK THAT WOULD SOLVE THE PROBLEM.

MIKEY, MIKEY, MIKEY...

I guess I do not see a problem...

WHY SHOULD I HAVE TO PAY NEW BOOK PRICES FOR A USED BOOK?

But they offered to reimburse you, right?

Mikey, think if it this way. What if the bookstore always had people bringing books back to them claiming that the book was not new after they had read it because there were obvious signs, like turning down pages as bookmarks? How would the bookstore really know if that was true?

I WOULD NEVER DO THAT!

You wouldn't, but there may be unscrupulous people that just might do that. If the bookstore took the approach to reimbursing people in this situation, I think that the situation would be a horrific problem, and the bookstore would lose money big time. I think it would cause bookstores that handled the problem in that manner to close their doors and go out of business. Remember that Meg Ryan and Tom Hanks movie, *You've Got Mail?* That was a similar situation, although that was somewhat different as Tom Hanks' new store was the reason Meg Ryan's shop lost so many customers.

Good point. Personally, we have seen a few bookstores go out of business due to the lack of business. People are not reading as much as they used to, methinks...

METHINKS?????

Just an expression, Wum. It really is a sad state of affairs. I think my favorite book of all time, is *Don Quixote, USA* by Richard Powell. Aside from the scriptures, of course.

OF COURSE.

WHY DID YOU LIKE IT SO MUCH? WE, AS A WHOLE PERSON HAVE READ IT, MANY TIMES OVER THE YEARS, BUT WE COULD NEVER UNDERSTAND WHY YOU LIKED IT SO MUCH.

Because the main character was so innocent, naïve, and trusting. It is a humorous look at a person who joins the Peace Corp and gets sent to the fictional Republic of San Marco in the Caribbean. He is sent there because his specialty in agriculture are bananas, and the San Marcans have the unique ability to 'grow one banana where two had grown before.' While there he gets involved with the rebels who are trying to revolt against the dictator, after the dictator tries to have him killed, yet not realizing that was the dictator's plan. His involvement with the rebels is in the manner of helping them to create food to feed all of the people, not realizing that the rebels are attempting to overthrow the dictator and establish a communistic style of government. The book is full of very subtle humor, and it pokes fun at a lot of stereotypes. It was written in 1966 and was the basis for a Woody Allen film called *Bananas* in 1971, I believe.

I THINK MY FAVORITE IS PRIDE AND PREJUDICE BY JANE AUSTEN. I THINK I FELL IN LOVE WITH ELIZABETH BENNET THE FIRST TIME I READ THE BOOK. THE LANGUAGE IS SUPERB, AND THE INTERACTION OF THE SEXES SHOWS ALL OF THE PITFALLS OF HUMAN RELATIONSHIPS. JUST A WONDERFUL BOOK.

THAT IS HOW I FEEL ABOUT SCOUT IN *TO KILL A MOCKINGBIRD*. THEN WHEN THE MOVIE CAME OUT IT CONFIRMED IT. COURSE I WAS JUST A PUP WHEN I READ IT, SO SHE SHOULDN'T HAVE TAKEN MY LOVE SO SERIOUSLY.

DUDE...IN THE MOVIE SHE WAS LIKE SIX OR SEVEN YEARS OLD! PERVERT!

YOU IDIOT! IT WAS NOTHING LIKE THAT. BESIDES, WHEN I FIRST READ THAT BOOK I WAS IN GRADE SCHOOL, AND I WAS TOO BUSY TRYING TO MAKE THE SCHOOL BASKETBALL TEAM. I DID, BUT AS YOU KNOW, WE WERE REALLY SHORT! I DIDN'T EVEN DISCOVER GIRLS UNTIL MY JUNIOR YEAR IN HIGH SCHOOL.

i think my favorite book is *lord jim* by joseph conrad. what a sad, sad book. it is about a man that makes a mistake early in life but leaves and becomes this great man in another area before his mistake catches up to him and destroys his life. bummer!

Well, this discussion went south in a hurry!

Then I guess it is up to me to bring it back to a higher level with my favorite book. It is *Man's Search for Meaning* by Victor Frankl. I am sure that we all remember it, and the reasons that Dad gave us the book to read at such an early age. I believe that it helped form our persona as it gave us the idea that we can think and be whatever it is that we desire. We, as in all of us, control our thoughts and actions, and therein lies the great freedom that Dr. Frankl was talking about, and why he felt that he was more free in a concentration camp than were his German guards. Quite a powerful book, if anyone remembers it...

I REMEMBER IT.

As do I.

me too.

ME THREE.

WHERE DID WE GET THIS GUY? CAN YOU REFRAIN FROM THE COMMENTS, PLEASE?

A LITTLE SLOW IN THE READING, BUT IT WAS A GOOD BOOK.

I WAS JUST GOING TO GIVE MY TWO CENTS WORTH ON MY FAVORITE BOOK. MAY I CONTINUE?

SORRY. TOO LATE. IT IS MY TURN. MY FAVORITE BOOK IS...DRUM ROLL PLEASE...*YEA WILDCATS* BY JOHN R. TUNIS. A FUN BOOK ABOUT BASKETBALL, NATURALLY, AND A COACH IN INDIANA THAT KICKS THE FIVE STARTERS OFF THE TEAM, IF I REMEMBER CORRECTLY. A GREAT STORY ABOUT ANGER, AND THE GOOD THAT CAN COME FROM IT!

THAT IS CERTAINLY IN LINE WITH YOUR LINE OF THINKING, MIKEY. VERY GOOD CHOICE! IT REALLY WAS A GOOD BOOK.

What person living in Indiana would NOT love a story about basketball!

CAN I GIVE MY INPUT ON MY FAVORITE BOOK?

IF WE HAVE TO LISTEN, I GUESS YOU CAN.

MY FAVORITE BOOK IS 'THE *BEST OF MAD MAGAZINE* BY THE EDITORS OF 'MAD' MAGAZINE...

That is not a real book. It is something 'Mad Magazine" puts out periodically to sell more magazines. Sort of like "The *Best of the 1910 Fruit Gum Company*" record album...

I am sorry, but there was no such record.

Actually, there was. It was put out in 2006.

Well, it should not have been, in my humble opinion...

I AGREE. BUT, *THE BEST OF MAD MAGAZINE* IS NOT A BOOK.

Actually, there are a whole bunch of books about Mad Magazine, and yes, some of them are titled the *Best of MAD Magazine*. A lot of them are compilations, but some of them are actually in book form. At least, that is what my sources tell me.

I guess it is only fitting that the last book we talk about is something that makes us all laugh, and Mad Magazine surely did that, when we read it years and years ago.

WELL, I GUESS WE KNOW WHO GOT THE LAST LAUGH ON THIS ONE!!!!!

I HATE THAT GUY!

me too!

I THINK THAT IF WE PUT IT TO A VOTE, IT WOULD BE UNANIMOUS!

Movies

("No good movie is too long, and no bad movie
is short enough." – Roger Ebert)

Author's Note: I would go to the movies on a daily basis if I could.
I enjoy them immensely and I always have. But like most people, if
I am in a certain mood or state of mind, then that would dictate the
type or genre of the movie that I would want to see. Hence, movies
are the perfect subject for discussion by the various aspects of my
persona. I hope you enjoy the discussion and the lists of MY favorite
movies.

Okay guys, listen up. Seeing that I am the one who spends most of our time in control of our body, I want to make a list of my favorite movies and see what you think. Sound good?

OKAY.

GREAT! I HAVE ALREADY STARTED MY LIST...

No, this is my show. No lists are allowed except mine.

did donald trump just join us?

Okay by me. Movies are a waste of time anyway.

WELL THEN, I GUESS YOU WILL NOT BE CONTRIBUTING ANY POWERFUL INSIGHTS FROM THAT OVERWORKED BRAIN OF YOURS, WILL YOU?

Of course. Just because I do not like movies does not necessarily mean I have nothing to contribute.

ARE WE GOING TO GO WITH CATEGORIES, GENRES, OR JUST THE FAVORITES?

Guys, you are making this too hard. You all know that I love movies. It is probably my second favorite thing to do in this world. I sometimes think that I should have done something in the movie business...

YOU STILL CAN. THE LOCAL THEATER IS LOOKING FOR AN USHER, TICKET TAKER, OR CLEAN UP GUY! BY THE WAY, WE ALL KNOW WHAT YOUR FAVORITE THING TO DO IS IN THE WORLD. OH MY GOSH, ARE YOU BLUSHING?

STAY ON POINT. GO AHEAD, MIKE.

Thanks, Michael. I am glad that at least one of you is in the right frame of mind. Let's start with my favorite movies, from my point of view.

whatever.

Here are my ten most favorite movies, in order. *Support Your Local Sheriff, The Great Race, Tombstone, The Apartment, It's a Mad, Mad, Mad, Mad World, Dr. Zhivago, The Sound of Music, Thoroughly Modern Millie, The Fifth Element,* and *Big Trouble.* What do you think?

WHERE IS *12 ANGRY MEN?*

WHERE IS *AIRPLANE?*

WHERE IS THE GODFATHER SERIES?

Where is *A Beautiful Mind?*

what about the magnificent seven?

AND *GODZILLA*...WHAT ABOUT THAT OUTSTANDING MOVIE?

Okay, I hear all of what you are saying, except for *Godzilla*. I admit, it is one of the somewhat unnerving in its lack of reality. However, it is a classic, I will admit that.

THANKS FOR THAT! I ACTUALLY DID NOT LIKE THE MOVIE. I WAS JUST MENTIONING IT BECAUSE THE OTHERS WERE MENTIONING MOVIES THAT MOST OF THE WORLD WOULD RECOGNIZE AS EXCELLENT MOVIES.

Well, Micky, I hate to burst your bubble, but we did watch *Godzilla* on the late show in the summer of 1966. Remember when we lived in the 2 bedroom apartment, and our sister was home from college, and we slept on a cot in front of the tv in the living room? Because of our back injury we could not work, therefore we spent the summer watching old movies until late at night or early in the morning. That is when we saw it.

YOU ARE CORRECT, DR. MIKE. I REMEMBER THAT... WHAT A GREAT FLICK!

Listen, there are so many movies, most of which I have not seen. Correction, that WE have not seen. I, we, have seen a lot of the movies since 1964, until the recent upsurge in "R" rated movies since 2010, so I think we have a pretty good basis for which are the best, or good, or bad, or whatever, so I suggest that we come up with our list, based upon what we have seen, and suggest that it is our opinion, and not the responsibility of the Oscar people, the Actor's Guild, or the Writer's Guild, or anyone else's. It is simply listings of a dedicated movie goer, and a self-confessed lover of movies. Agreed?

sounds good, but are we allowed to disagree, and tell you that you are such a geek and a moron for the choices that you make?

No, but you may say why you think my choices are in error.

i will refrain from speaking, then, because this sounds like no fun whatsoever!

SUIT YOURSELF, MR. MIKE, BUT I THINK MIKE IS RIGHT. BUT, I DO THINK IT IS WISE TO SEPARATE THE LISTS INTO DIFFERENT GENRES, SUCH AS COMEDY, WESTERN, DRAMA, ROMANCE, ACTION, ADVENTURE, FANTASY, AND MUSICAL. AFTER ALL THAT WOULD ALLOW US TO PRAISE MORE MOVIES, AND PEOPLE MIGHT APPRECIATE OUR INCLUSION OF THEIR FAVORITE MOVIE.

But, what about movies that may be a combination of multiple genres? Such as *"Cat Ballou".* It is a western, but obviously a comedic entry also.

AT THE END OF THE DISCUSSION, YOU CHOOSE YOUR 10 BEST LIST FROM THE OTHER LIST, BUT ALSO SUGGEST THAT THEY ARE INCLUDED IN MORE THAN ONE GENRE.

Okey dokey. Let's start with Comedy. My 15 Best Comedies are, in order: *Support Your Local Sheriff, It's a Mad, Mad, Mad, Mad World, Blazing Saddles, Big Trouble, Spaceballs, Ferris Bueller's Day Off, It Happened One Night, M*A*S*H, Airplane!, The Star Spangled Girl, The Odd Couple, A Fish Called Wanda, Mr. Mom, The Producers,* and *Brewster's Millions.*

Are you serious? Man, do we have a weird sense of humor?

THERE IS NOTHING WRONG WITH OUR SENSE OF HUMOR!

LET'S MOVE ON, SHALL WE?

Certainly. Best westerns are as follows: *The Magnificent Seven, Support Your Local Sheriff, Blazing Saddles, The Good the Bad and the Ugly, A Fistful of Dollars, For a Few Dollars More, Shane, The Quick and the Dead, How The West Was Won, El Dorado, Cat Ballou, The Gunfighter, Hang Em High, Maverick,* and *The Fastest Gun In The West.*

A LITTLE CLINT EASTWOOD BIAS, EH? I WOULD ARGUE ABOUT A FEW OF YOUR CHOICES.

Like?

EL DORADO, FOR ONE. THE ONLY THING GOOD ABOUT THAT MOVIE WAS A YOUNG MICHELLE CAREY! ON THE NEGATIVE SIDE YOU HAD A YOUNG JAMES CAAN (TOTALLY MISCAST), THEN MAKING A HORSE'S REAR END WITH HIS POLITICALLY

INCORRECT 'IMPRESSION' OF A PERSON OF CHINESE ANCESTRY. THEN YOU HAD ED ASNER AND CHRISTOPHER GEORGE AS VILLAINS, BOTH SERIOUSLY MISCAST. OF COURSE, YOU HAD ROBERT MITCHUM AND JOHN WAYNE WHO, STRANGELY ENOUGH, ACTUALLY DID PRETTY GOOD ACTING JOBS. THE WRITING WAS ALSO VERY WEAK. OTHER THAN THOSE LITTLE ISSUES, I WOULD AGREE THAT IT WAS A GREAT MOVIE.

WOW! WHAT DID YOU REALLY THINK OF THE MOVIE, MICHAEL?

can we move along? i have some thoughts on other categories...

Maybe we just better save those lists for another time. I am not sure my ego can stand any more criticism.

If you are this sensitive about 'suggestions' from us, what are you going to do when people read this book, and offer 'suggestions'?

I wasn't going to publish our conversations as a book. I was just going to put it into a time capsule, and let my progenitors think about it in 200 years.

WHY?

Wouldn't you like to know what our ancestors thought about, and were like 200 years ago?

IF I HAD SHOWN THAT INTEREST, WOULDN'T I BE MORE INTERESTED IN DOING GENEALOGY?

Point taken. Tell you what...how about I publish our conversations as a book, and then if people like it, I can write more books about movies, songs, and some of our random thoughts. What do you think of that?

you are kidding, of course?

I THINK IT IS A GREAT IDEA. LET US ALL SHOW THE WORLD OUR INNER MOST THOUGHTS...I AM SURE IT WILL BE A BEST SELLER.

IT PROBABLY WILL. THERE ARE A LOT OF NEUROTIC PEOPLE OUT THERE!

I am not sure that is a good idea. Most writers do not get published. Can we stand one more disappointment in our life?

AS LONG AS WE DO NOT HAVE TO SEE THE MOVIE MAMA MIA, OR THE SEQUEL, I CAN STAND ANOTHER DISAPPOINTMENT.

You guys are sick. No wonder I love to watch movies...I get to get away from you guys!

God

("Most people wish to serve God – but only in
an advisory capacity." Author Unknown)

Author's Note: I had a few philosophy classes when I was in college,
and to me they were intriguing. The arguments for and against
the existence of a creator were primarily built upon the intellectual
capabilities of the professors. My experience taught me much of the
basis of this last discussion. But I must confess that my belief in the
existence of a creator was given to me by my parents, and fortified
by years of trial, error, belief, faith, and hope.

Michael…are you there?

OF COURSE. I AM ALWAYS HERE. WHAT IS GOING ON?

I have a question. Is there a God?

YES.

How do you know?

I SUPPOSE I COULD SAY THAT ALL OF THE EXPERIENCES THAT WE HAVE GONE THROUGH, AND ALL THAT I KNOW, AND READ ABOUT, AND THOUGHT ABOUT HAS LED ME TO BELIEVE THAT THERE IS A GOD.

What about those people who say that there is no God, or that He is dead?

I DO NOT BELIEVE THAT WE, AS HUMAN BEINGS ON THIS EARTH, HAVE THE SUM TOTAL OF THE KNOWLEDGE THAT EXISTS IN THE UNIVERSE. PART OF THE FASCINATING GROWTH OF THE HUMAN FAMILY HAS BEEN THE INCREDIBLE INCREASE IN OUR KNOWLEDGE OVER THE PAST 50 YEARS, WITH THE INCREASES IN TECHNOLOGY, ETC. IT IS ASTOUNDING WHAT HAS HAPPENED OVER THE PAST 50 YEARS! I WOULD ASK THE ATHEIST/AGNOSTIC IF THERE HAS BEEN ANY INCREASE IN HUMAN KNOWLEDGE OVER THAT TIME.

Obviously there has…

PRECISELY! THAT WOULD LEAD ME TO THE CONCLUSION THAT THE KNOWLEDGE THAT WE AS HUMANS DO NOT HAVE THE SUM TOTAL OF ALL THE KNOWLEDGE OF THE UNIVERSE. BY MAKING THAT ASSUMPTION, YOU AUTOMATICALLY RECOGNIZE THAT THERE ARE THINGS THAT WE HUMANS

DO NOT KNOW, AND THAT MAY INCLUDE THE KNOWLEDGE OF GOD.

But there are people who still insist that there is no god.

TO SUGGEST THAT WE HAVE THE SUM TOTAL OF ALL KNOWLEDGE IN THE UNIVERSE BY STATING THAT THERE IS NO GOD IS AN EPITOME OF HUMAN ARROGANCE, AND I DISAGREE MOST STRIDENTLY WITH THAT PREMISE. THAT IS THEIR CHOICE. BUT I BELIEVE THAT THERE IS MUCH MORE EVIDENCE TO PROVE THE EXISTENCE OF GOD THAN TO DENY HIS EXISTENCE.

Such as...

YOU ARE STANDING UPON IT, MY FRIEND. LOOK AT THIS WORLD, AND ALL THAT IS IN IT, INCLUDING WE HUMANS. ALL OF IT CRIES OUT TO ME THAT THERE IS A GOD! LOOK AT A NEWBORN BABY...IS THERE ANY GREATER PROOF NEEDED? LOOK AT US HUMANS. HOW WE CAN GROW, AND DEVELOP, AND THINK, AND REASON, AND MAKE MISTAKES, AND CORRECT THOSE MISTAKES. ALL OF THIS TELLS ME, ALONG WITH A WHOLE BUNCH OF OTHER THINGS, THAT NOT ONLY THAT THERE IS A GOD, BUT HE LOVES US, AND IS ALSO VERY CONCERNED ABOUT US AS A PEOPLE, AND AS INDIVIDUALS.

How so?

I DO NOT THINK GOD JUST CREATED THIS EARTH AND PLACED US UPON IT, THEN LETS US GO ON OUR MERRY LITTLE WAY. I BELIEVE THAT HE IS WATCHING OVER US, AND THAT HE HAS A PLAN FOR EACH OF US HUMANS, AND HOW WE LIVE ACCORDING TO HIS DICTATES IS GOING TO DETERMINE OUR

FATES IN THE LIFE TO COME. HE CARES ABOUT US. WE ARE HIS CHILDREN.

So, there is a life after this one? That is what I have been taught all of my life. I have always believed that, but so few others believe it, I was beginning to wonder if it just wishful thinking. I also have been taught, as you know, that there is a life, a SPIRITUAL life prior to this one, where we existed.

YES, THAT IS TRUE. ONCE YOU RECOGNIZE THE FULL EXISTENCE OF THE HUMAN SPIRIT, YOU GET THE FULL GLIMPSE OF A GOD WHO IS A 'FATHER' AND NOT JUST A CREATOR. AS A FATHER IN HEAVEN, HE IS MOST ACUTELY AWARE OF HIS CHILDREN, AND WHAT THEY ARE DOING TO HIS WORLD, AND TO HIS CHILDREN.

if god is so concerned about his children, why is there so much pain and suffering in this world? couldn't he make it easier for all concerned?

I DO NOT KNOW THE ANSWER TO THAT QUESTION, EXCEPT THAT I BELIEVE THAT WHAT HAPPENS TO US IS DUE TO THE CIRCUMSTANCES WE CHOOSE. FOR EXAMPLE, IF YOU DECIDE TO ROB A BANK, AND YOU DO, AND THEN YOU GET CAUGHT, YOU ARE PROBABLY GOING TO JAIL. WAS THAT DUE TO GOD, OR YOUR OWN CHOICES?

obviously, my choice, but what about the baby that dies after a few days of life? where was god in that one?

THINK OF IT THIS WAY...WHAT IF GOD IS SO TUNED IN TO OUR LIVES THAT HE KNOWS EVERYTHING THAT IS GOING TO HAPPEN TO ALL OF US, EVEN THE BABY THAT DIES A FEW WEEKS AFTER BEING BORN. WHAT IF, IN ADDITION,

HE CREATED ALL OF US AND LIVES WITH US, SPIRITUALLY, BEFORE WE CAME HERE MORTALLY TO THIS EARTH. THEN WE KNEW HIM TO BE A KIND, LOVING FATHER AND WE FOLLOWED HIS ADVICE TO COME HERE TO, IN A SENSE, LEARN TO LIVE AND LOVE HIM IN FAITH. THEN THERE ARE ALSO CERTAIN THINGS THAT WE NEED TO EXPERIENCE AND LEARN TO CONTROL IN MORTALITY, SUCH AS PATIENCE...

I HEARD THAT! ARE YOU SAYING THAT I NEED TO LEARN MORE PATIENCE?

WELL, IF THE SHOE FITS...

GENTLEMEN, AND I USE THE TERM VERY LOOSELY, KNOCK IT OFF. WHAT I AM SAYING IS THAT IN THIS SPHERE IN WHICH WE FIND OURSELVES, THERE ARE A LOT OF QUESTIONS THAT, QUITE FRANKLY, ARE UNANSWERABLE AND OUT OF THE REALM OF OUR THINKING.

But, wait a minute. Let's get back to the baby that dies. Are you saying it was God's will that the baby dies?

WHAT IF THIS BABY WAS SO GOOD AND WONDERFUL, AND SO PURE, THAT ALL THE SPIRIT NEEDED WAS TO EXPERIENCE A BIRTH IN THE MORTAL WORLD, I.E., TO GAIN A 'BODY' THAT WILL BE HIS IN THE RESURRECTION. IN A SENSE, THIS BABY WAS SO GOOD AND PURE THAT THE BABY HAD ALREADY 'EARNED' THE PROMISE THAT GOD HAS MADE TO ALL OF US, IF WE DO WHAT HE WANTS US TO DO, AND NOT WHAT WE WANT TO DO. THEN, THE BABY DID NOT NEED THE EXPERIENCES OF MORTALITY, BUT WENT BACK TO THE GOD THAT GAVE LIFE IN THE FIRST PLACE. THAT WAS ALL THAT THE BABY NEEDED.

So, in a sense, babies that pass away are going back to God that gave them life in the first place, not as a penalty, but as a choice son or daughter that did not have to 'prove' his or her worthiness.

EXACTLY.

but what about the parents? is this experience a 'joyful' experience, then, or is it a horrible outcome of a long anticipated, and hoped for, event? i can't believe that they would be happy.

I would think that they would be very unhappy and sad, unless they had the understanding that you are suggesting. I know people who have had that experience both with an 'understanding' and without. The couple that had this belief and understanding were sad, but they were confident that God was in His Plan, and they were happy and content. The other couple turned away from God, continued in their grief, and later had a child.

WHAT DO YOU THINK ABOUT HOW GOD FEELS WHEN THESE THINGS HAPPEN? IS HE SAD FOR US, AND DOES HE COMFORT US WHEN ASKED? IF HE LOVES US AND CARES FOR US AS MUCH AS I THINK HE DOES, HE CERTAINLY IS GOING TO HELP HIS CHILDREN WHENEVER THEY ASK HIM TO, JUST LIKE AN EARTHLY PARENT. IT REALLY DOES COME DOWN TO WHAT WE BELIEVE, WHAT WE FEEL, AND WHAT WE BELIEVE ABOUT OUR EXISTENCE HERE, WHERE WE COME FROM, AND WHERE DO WE GO FROM HERE.

So, we are in control of our own destinies, so to speak.

YES, IN EVERY SENSE OF THE WORD BUT ONE. BECAUSE WE ARE NOT PERFECT, AND WE DO MAKE MISTAKES, THERE HAS TO BE SOME MECHANISM WHEREBY OUR SINS ARE FORGIVEN SO THAT WE CAN RETURN TO FATHER AND LIVE WITH HIM AGAIN.

why?

Because God is perfect. He is without sin. Correct?

CORRECT. THE SCRIPTURES STATE THAT GOD CANNOT LOOK UPON SIN 'WITH THE LEAST DEGREE OF ALLOWANCE.'(DOCTRINE AND COVENANTS 1:31) THEREFORE WE CAN ASSUME THAT HE WOULD WANT US ALL TO BE FREE FROM SIN, AND SINCE WE DO SIN, HOW IS THAT TO BE ACCOMPLISHED? THROUGH THE SACRIFICE OF HIS PERFECT SON, JESUS CHRIST. HE HAS PAID FOR ALL OF OUR SINS, IF WE BELIEVE IN HIM, EXERCISE FAITH AND REPENT OF THE THINGS THAT WE HAVE DONE WRONG, I.E., OUR SINS.

But what of the people of the world who do not believe in Jesus? We are talking about a lot of the people currently in the world who may have heard of Jesus, but are of other religions or non-religious. What about those people?

I think they will have the opportunity to learn about Jesus and accept Him in the next life.

there are some people who believe that unless you commit to jesus in this life, you will be in hell.

Even if you die with never having heard the name?

yup.

Even a baby that dies two minutes after being born?

i guess so.

I do not believe that is something a merciful and loving God would do. That does not make sense to me.

THERE ARE SOME WHO WOULD MAKE THE SAME ARGUMENT FOR NOT BELIEVING IN GOD.

I have had discussions with people of all faiths/religions and with some agnostics, and yes, even some atheists. It just seems to me that we will not know the absolute answer to the question "Does God Exist?" until we die. But, if I believe in Him, can I know in this life that He exists, or will I have to wait until I die?

I BELIEVE THAT YOU CAN. WE HAVE DONE THAT, AND I HAVE RECEIVED A WITNESS THAT HE DOES EXIST. I FEEL COMFORTABLE WITH THAT SCENARIO.

Me too. Although, I do think that there are going to be a lot of surprised people in the next life.

i just hope i am not one them.

Me too.

BINGO!

I agree.

HERE'S HOPING!

I THINK WE WILL BE OKAY. JUST BE PATIENT AND LIVE THE WAY HE WOULD WANT YOU TO LIVE.

YOU JUST HAD TO PUT IN THE P-WORD DIDN'T YOU?

unless someone cleans up his language, and becomes more patient, we may not make it!

OOPS! WE HAVE MET THE ENEMY, AND HE IS US!

CPSIA information can be obtained
at www.ICGtesting.com
Printed in the USA
LVHW101647040122
707832LV00018B/776/J

9 781532 087042